FORGOTTEN

Driving home in the dark, Serena stops to help an injured man lying in a ditch. He mutters something unintelligible, but that is only the start of her problems. Someone is watching the apartment she shares with her brother, her mother is being particularly secretive, and police detective Jack Armstrong is convinced Serena is hiding something. Just when she thinks things can get no worse, her missing father turns up. This is definitely not the time to fall in love.

FAY CUNNINGHAM

FORGOTTEN

Complete and Unabridged

LINFORD
Leicester

First published in Great Britain in 2013

First Linford Edition
published 2014

A catalogue record for this book is available
from the British Library.

ISBN 978–1–4448–2079–9

Published by
F. A. Thorpe (Publishing)
Anstey, Leicestershire

Set by Words & Graphics Ltd.
Anstey, Leicestershire
Printed and bound in Great Britain by
T. J. International Ltd., Padstow, Cornwall

This book is printed on acid-free paper

1

The sudden thud jerked her into full attentiveness, adrenaline pulsing through her veins.

Had she hit something?

There had been a shadow in the headlights for a second, insubstantial, like a loose bundle of rags blown by the wind. But whatever it was had hit the front of her car.

Damn!

She sat still for a moment, undecided, the engine still running. Whether to just drive on or whether to check if there was any damage to the car. She couldn't sit in the middle of the road, so she put the car into gear and pulled onto the grass verge, stopping just before she drove into the ditch.

It was so damned dark.

Leaving her headlights on, she climbed reluctantly out of the car, taking her mobile phone with her. She wanted to call Simon, but if she woke him up he would kill her.

The front of the car looked fine, but it was difficult to see, the lights were blinding her. Holding the phone in one hand, she ran her other hand over the plastic bumper. There didn't seem to be any dents, just something wet and sticky. She held her hand in the beam from one of the headlights.

Her palm was smeared with what looked suspiciously like blood.

With a little gasp, she moved away from the lights, bending down to rub her hand frantically in the damp grass. An animal? It must have been an animal, but she hadn't hit it hard, just a little bump. She rubbed her hand in the grass again. Why wasn't she one of those people who always carried wet wipes with them?

Now she really did want to phone Simon. She even got as far as tapping in the number, but then she thought of his cross voice on the other end of the line and cancelled the call. It was probably just a rabbit. Rabbits were all over the road at this time of night. She refused to acknowledge the fact that the blood on her bumper was a good eighteen inches above road level.

She reached back into the car for the tiny pocket torch she always carried under the dash and, thus armed, flashlight in one hand, phone in the other, started back up the lane. She couldn't leave an animal lying in the road badly injured, even a rabbit.

It was like walking into a black hole. An owl hooted, making her jump, and nameless things rustled in the bushes. She used the torch like a metal detector, sweeping it from side to side in front of her. Her shoes weren't made for walking and her skirt was too tight, clutching at her knees with every step. This was just plain stupid. She swung the beam around in a circle. Nothing. Time to go home.

She was about to start back when she heard a noise. She felt her ears move as she listened, straining to hear any tiny sound. A moment later she heard something up ahead making strange noises. She hitched up her skirt and hobbled the last few yards. In the beam of the flashlight she could see a dark shape half in, half out of the ditch. Something large and raggedy. She bent down.

And a face stared up at her.

At least, it looked like a face. She had dropped the flashlight in her panic and could only guess it was human. It certainly wasn't a rabbit.

She wanted so badly to scream. It was like one of those awful dreams where you open your mouth and no sound comes out. All she could produce was a little squeak. Had she done this? Hit someone hard enough to toss them into a ditch like a broken doll?

'I can't have done this,' she whimpered. 'Please don't let me have done this.' She bent down again. 'It's all right,' she said stupidly, knowing it

4

wasn't. 'I'll get help. I've got a cell phone.'

For a moment she couldn't remember what she had done with the phone, but it was still clutched firmly in her left hand. She moved it around, trying to get a signal. The dial was startlingly green in the darkness. Searching . . . the dial said, searching . . .

She waved the handset around desperately. One little blip — now two. That would have to be enough. She tried to dial, all fumbling fingers, and nearly dialled 911, remembering at the last minute that the emergency number was 999. Then a woman answered, talking ridiculously slowly.

Where was she? How was she supposed know? All these little lanes looked the same.

What were the landmarks?

Stupid woman. What landmarks? It was dark, for goodness sake. She tried to recall the signpost for the last village she had come through. Langtree, or something similar. 'And my lights are on,' she told them. 'Please hurry.'

She found her flashlight and blundered down the bank, almost falling into the ditch beside the injured man. She guessed it was a man because his hair was cropped short and he was wearing a polo shirt. His eyes had been shut, but suddenly they popped open and he stared straight at her. She jumped back with another squeal. His lips were moving as he tried to tell her something, so she squatted down beside him, trying to make out individual words, but it was hopeless. The few words she did understand didn't make any sense and his mouth was so swollen it was obviously painful for him to speak.

'Don't talk,' she whispered, but he caught hold of her hand.

'What happened?' His voice sounded like a croak, almost inaudible.

She looked at him helplessly. 'I don't know. I think I hit you with my car. I'm so sorry.'

His hand tightened on hers. 'Remember number. Important.'

Still clutching her hand, he mumbled some numbers. She tried to memorise them, thinking they might be a telephone number, but wasn't sure she heard them correctly. When she tried to release her hand he wouldn't let go.

'Help me . . . please.'

A damp ditch was probably not the best place for an accident victim so she helped him crawl onto the grass bank. He managed to prop himself up in a half-sitting position, and for the first time she realised how young he was.

'Where do you hurt?'

He touched his arm and she saw he was holding his arm awkwardly. She thought it might be broken.

'You shouldn't move,' she shone her torch. 'You've got a gash on the side of your head. I think all the blood on you must have come from there. Heads always bleed a lot. Have you got a handkerchief?'

When he didn't answer she realised he was slipping in and out of consciousness. Further up the lane, headlights were coming fast towards them. Serena breathed a sigh of relief and flashed her torch in the direction of the lights. This must be the ambulance. 'Hang on a bit longer, please,' she whispered, more to herself than to him.

But the car that screeched to a stop beside them wasn't an ambulance. The passenger door shot open and a man leapt out. He looked back over his shoulder at the driver. 'There's a woman as well. What do you want me to do?'

Serena frowned. The man was short and stocky and he looked quite menacing. 'You're not paramedics, are you? Where's the ambulance?'

The driver got out slowly and walked round the car towards her. He was taller and thinner than his passenger.

'Police. Plain clothes. We picked up your call and we were nearby. We can take the victim to hospital. It'll be quicker in the long run.'

Police. That explained the menacing look — and the word victim. But she didn't like the look of either of them. She glanced down at the man sitting at her feet. 'Do you want to go with them?'

He shook his head. 'No!' He obviously didn't want to go with the men in the car and the single word he'd managed to gasp out had been filled with panic, but she knew he needed to get to hospital as quickly as possible. As she stood, undecided, one of policeman took a step towards the injured man. 'I need a hand here,' he said, looking at his companion.

'Wait,' she held up her hand. 'He doesn't want to go with you, and the ambulance will be here in a minute.'

The tall man looked as if he was about to say something, but at that minute an ambulance came round the corner, lights flashing, and pulled to a halt beside Serena's car.

The man hesitated, then he looked at his partner and shook his head. The two of them ran back to their car and drove off just as a paramedic got out of the ambulance. He dropped to his knees beside the injured man and another man followed, carrying a bag. Within seconds they had fitted a mask over the young man's face, set up a drip, and popped him on a stretcher. The police car that followed the ambulance a few minutes later disgorged two tired-looking policemen.

How many policemen does it take to sort out one traffic accident? Serena wondered. It sounded like the start of a joke.

They made their way ponderously towards her, stopping to talk to the ambulance crew before they examined her car, shining a torch on the front, and then bending down to look underneath. One of them reached inside to turn off her headlights. They were fainter now, the battery running down.

She was sitting on a rug on the bank, trying to stop her knees banging together. The ambulance driver had told her to sit down; someone would be with her in a minute. Her face was streaked with tears, her hair had come loose from its clips and hung down in untidy curls, and somewhere she seemed to have lost a shoe. The paramedics were still working on the man, trying to assess his injuries and stabilise him before taking him to the local hospital.

'Could we have your name, miss, please?' one of the policemen asked. She hadn't noticed him come up beside her.

'Serena. Serena Conti.'

He looked up from his notebook, taking in the dark hair and even darker eyes. Like the name, a gift from her absent father.

'Italian?'

'No. American.'

He licked the point of his pencil and made a note on his pad. 'Thought the accent wasn't Italian. And your address?'

She gave him the address and watched him write it down.

'I got lost on my way home. I'm staying with Simon Prescott. He's English. He lives here. In England.'

She was gabbling, suddenly very tired. 'Can I go now, please?'

'Are you hurt? Do you need someone to look at you?'

She shook her head. 'No, it's not my blood.'

The younger policeman had been talking to the paramedics. Now he nodded towards the ambulance. 'You won't get a statement from that one for a while. He looks as if he's been run over by a steamroller. What did you do to him? Reverse back over him a few times?'

Serena tried to hold her knees still. 'It was just a little bump,' she said in a small voice. 'I don't know how he got like that.'

'We'll do a breathalyser, anyway, shall we? Just to be on the safe side.'

She worried about the glass of wine at lunch, but that was nearly twelve hours ago. All the same, she wished she

hadn't drunk it. Would her antihista-
mine tablets affect the result? What if
she was over the limit? Could they have
her for manslaughter?

The breathalyser was clear, but they
refused to let her drive, so she travelled
home in the police car with the second
man following in her hire car. She
wondered fleetingly if he was insured to
drive it, her firm was very hot on things
like that. They parked her car outside
Simon's apartment block and asked her
again if she was all right. She assured
them she was. The last thing she wanted
was for a couple of policemen to escort
her indoors and wake Simon. They saw
her into the lift and then drove off.

She turned the key in the lock almost
reluctantly. Simon's apartment never
felt like home, but living at home had
never been easy, either. When she had
been offered the trip to England, she
had left the battle zone that living with
her mother entailed, and gratefully
moved in with Simon for a few weeks.

Once inside, she didn't turn on any

lights until she was safely in the bathroom — and then wished she hadn't. Her white blouse was stained all down the front, and her hair was matted together with twigs and leaves and God knows what else. She shuddered and stripped off, running the shower so hot it scalded her. It took half a bottle of shampoo to get her hair clean. Wrapping herself in a towel, she stuffed her stained clothing down at very the bottom of the laundry basket where Simon wouldn't see it. She had to tell him sometime, but not tonight.

In the living room the answer machine light was flashing. She turned the sound down low and curled up on the sofa to listen to the messages. She was utterly exhausted, but she knew sleep wouldn't come yet, and she couldn't go to bed without listening to her calls. She never could. She was afraid she might miss something important.

Three of the messages were for Simon, two about business, and one an invitation for him to play golf the following Sunday. One message was from her mother — 'Are you dead, Serena? Or don't you want to talk to me?'

'I don't want to talk to you, mother,' she told the machine.

The last message was from the local branch of her firm asking her why she hadn't called in.

'Because I got lost and nearly killed someone.' If she hadn't got lost, she reminded herself, she wouldn't have hit the man on the road.

When she eventually climbed into bed it was gone midnight, and when she awoke in the morning Simon had already left for work.

She phoned in and took the day off sick. After all, it was a Friday.

* * *

She was doing a bit of housekeeping when the detective arrived. Pushing the vacuum cleaner hard, panting with the exertion, chasing non-existent bits of fluff round Simon's navy blue carpet and trying to keep her mind off the previous night. She kept telling herself it was all a bad dream, but her blood-stained clothes still sat in the laundry basket, waiting for her to pluck up the courage to get them out and put them in the wash.

She turned off the vacuum cleaner and stood in the middle of the room, sweating. She was wearing a sports top and a pair of cotton shorts. Her hair was clean now, tied in a precarious knot on top of her head. Little ringlets had escaped and stuck to her damp face and forehead. She had no makeup on and her feet were bare.

The sound of the doorbell startled her.

She went to the front door and peered through the spy hole. Not someone she knew. He was turned away from her, his fingers tapping impatiently on the door. He must be a colleague of Simon's. She looked down at her bare feet. Oh, well, she could always pretend she was the cleaning woman. She opened the door a few inches.

'Miss Conti?'

She nodded, wondering how he knew her name.

'I'm Detective Inspector Jack Armstrong. May I come in?'

Her heart did a little flip. They had told her someone would come for a statement. Was she supposed to have something written out? She wondered if she ought to ask for ID. He certainly didn't look like a policeman. He wasn't wearing uniform, just blue jeans and a black polo shirt, and his dark hair was a bit too long for a regular policeman. Before she could say anything he held up his ID.

'You'd better come in.'

He was tall, and ducked automatically as he came through the doorway. She watched him make a quick assessment of the living room; taking in the navy carpet and curtains, the two black leather sofas, and the limited edition Hockney on the wall.

The bright yellow cushions had been her idea. Simon didn't really like them.

She waved a hand at one of the sofas, but he didn't sit down. Instead, he walked across the room and stared at the picture.

'It was chosen to match the curtains,' Serena offered helpfully. When he didn't reply she could contain herself no longer. 'The man I hit, is he still alive?'

Jack Armstrong turned and looked at her, his eyes appraising. They were a surprisingly light blue, unusual with that dark hair.

'Just about. Someone gave him a thorough beating and dumped him in the ditch. Left him for dead. He must have come to and been staggering about in the road when you hit him.'

Serena took a long, slow breath.

'You mean, it wasn't me who mangled him up like that?'

'You probably didn't do him a lot of good when you hit him with your car and tossed him back in the ditch. The poor chap had probably only just crawled out. But no, the worst of the damage was already done.' He stared at her for a few moments until she looked away. 'What did he say to you?'

Serena didn't like this man. He had the coolest eyes she had ever seen — and he was treating her like a suspect.

'I don't know what you mean,' she said.

'Oh, I'm sure you do. Take time to think, if you want. You said he was conscious when you found him — and mumbling. In my book, mumbling means saying something. He had no identification on him and we need to know who he is. So . . . ' this time he took out a notebook, ' . . . exactly what did he say to you?'

What was this, the Spanish inquisition? 'Shouldn't you take me down to the police station if you're going to question me?'

He snapped his notebook shut. 'Your

choice. I thought it would be easier here, but if that's what you want.'

He was halfway to the door before she realised she had talked herself into a trap.

'Wait a minute . . . ' she waved her hands in the air. 'Yes, he did say something, but I don't know what. Like I said, he was mumbling.' She tried to think. 'He said 'phone' and something like 'left', and he muttered a few things I didn't catch. That's about it, I think.'

She wasn't going to tell Jack Armstrong about the numbers. She needed to check with the injured man. She wasn't even sure she'd heard right.

The detective didn't answer straight away. Instead, he drew in his cheeks, running his eyes from the top of her head to the tip of her toes.

'The accent. It's not Italian.'

'No.'

'Is this your permanent address?'

'No. I work for a marketing company and I'm over here on business. It is legal.'

'Oh, I'm sure. And the flat belongs to the boyfriend?'

What business was it of his? She decided not to answer. Let him think what he liked. Instead, she gave him the same appraising look he had given her. He wasn't bad looking, actually. Tall, dark, and with a certain arrogance that was quite attractive, even though it was annoying.

When he realised she wasn't going to reply, he handed her a card. 'Call me if you think of anything else. If he has family, they need to know how sick he is. We're checking his fingerprints, but he had no identity on him, none at all. Mr Nobody in person.' He smiled at her briefly. 'Don't worry too much, Miss Conti. The doctors think he's going to live.'

2

Serena let him out and then ran to the window to see if she could identify his car. She had discovered you can tell a lot about a man by the car he drives, but by the time she got to the window he was turning out on to the road. She was pretty certain he wasn't driving a regulation police car.

On impulse, she rang the number on the card he had given her to check. Yes, it was the main police station for the area and, yes, Detective Inspector Jack Armstrong did work there.

She tried to get back into her bout of cleaning, but somehow she'd lost the incentive. She took the bloodied clothes out of the bin and put her blouse in the washing machine. Her suit would have to go to the dry cleaners, and she had no idea how she was going to explain the stains.

She could imagine the conversation.

'What exactly have you spilt on your jacket, madam?'

'Rather a lot of blood, I'm afraid, but it isn't mine.'

She wished she could afford to throw them all away, some of the blood had even soaked through to her underwear, but money was too tight for that sort of extravagance, even with expenses. She was just trying to decide whether she could afford to ditch her bra, when the telephone rang.

'Miss Conti?'

'Yes,' she answered warily. She didn't recognise the voice.

'This is Kate Brennan from the Essex Post. Can you give me any information on the accident you were involved in last night? I believe you saved a man's life. Is that correct?'

'No, I didn't save his life.' How had they got that idea? 'He was in a ditch by the road. I called an ambulance, that's all.'

'My informant at the hospital tells

me if you hadn't called for help so quickly, the man would have died. I understand he was semi-conscious. Did he speak to you at all?'

'Not really. Just a few words.'

'What exactly did he say?'

Serena had been asked that same question only an hour ago. It was probably time she shut up.

'I'm sorry,' she said politely, 'but the police have asked me not to talk to the press. Goodbye.' She put the phone down with a worried frown. This was getting out of hand. She had to tell Simon what had happened. If this got in the papers he would go mad. Thank goodness they didn't know she had knocked the poor man in the ditch in the first place. As it was, they had her down as some sort of heroine. Talk about smelling of roses.

She decided to spend the rest of the day shopping to cheer herself up.

★　★　★

The story was in the papers the next morning, together with a photo that must have been copied from a company magazine, and Simon was not impressed.

'What you don't seem to realise, Serena, is how this might affect my work. I have a respected position in the City. Any sort of scandal . . .'

He was an attorney, for goodness sake, a solicitor, not Judge Dredd. 'What scandal? All I did was stop and help someone.' She crossed her fingers behind her back. 'Some poor man who'd been knocked down by a car.'

'Not according to the paper.' He waved it under her nose. 'According to this, the man had been beaten up prior to being dumped. There is talk of Mafia involvement. Perhaps a drugs deal gone wrong. Haven't you read the article?'

Serena shook her head. She hadn't had the chance. Simon always grabbed the paper first.

'You should keep out of things like this while you're living with me.'

'You would have just driven on, I suppose.'

'I would have stayed in the car and called for help. That would have been sensible.'

She couldn't tell Simon why she was out of her car without admitting she had knocked the man into the ditch. Oh, what a tangled web we weave, she thought miserably.

Simon was her half-brother, and insufferably British. Unlike her, he had been born in wedlock. He had an English father who had died a few years ago. Serena didn't know anything about her own father, and her mother wasn't talking.

Just after Simon left for a round of Saturday golf, the phone rang.

Serena hoped it wasn't the newspaper again. She was just about to go out.

'Yes?' she said, holding the phone on her shoulder while she hunted in her bag for her car keys.

'Jack Armstrong.'

His voice raised all the little hairs

along the backs of her arms and she hated it when that happened.

'Yes?' she said again, rather sharply. Where on earth had she put her keys? She took the phone away from her ear and stared around the room in exasperation. They must be somewhere. She could hear noises coming from the telephone. The darn man was shouting at her.

'I have to go out,' she shouted back at him. 'I can't talk to you now.' She was planning on visiting the hospital where they'd taken the mystery man, but she wasn't going to tell him that.

'I'm just leaving the station.'

'The police station?'

'No, the railway station,' he said sarcastically. 'Our nameless victim is asking for you.'

'Me?'

'Goodness me, this is going to take quite a while, isn't it? Yesterday you appeared quite intelligent.'

'I have to go out, Mr Armstrong,' she said through gritted teeth.

'This is police business. The victim is conscious and wants to talk to you, and I need to be with you when he does.' He paused, waiting for her to answer. When she didn't, he said, 'What part of that didn't you understand? Perhaps I can phrase it more simply.'

Serena decided she really hated this man. 'I'll see you at the hospital in half an hour,' she said. Her teeth were beginning to hurt with all the gritting.

'No. I'll pick you up. Ten minutes.'

She was about to tell him she didn't take orders, but he'd hung up. She took a couple of deep breaths. No point in getting all worked up over nothing.

He was driving a black Saab 900 with the top down and she looked at it uncertainly. 'It looks like rain.'

'I bet your glass is always half-empty. If it rains, I'll put the top up. There were no pool cars available, so please get in Miss Conti, or we'll be standing here all day.'

'This is your own car?'

'Suppose I answer the rest of your

questions while I drive.' He swung open the car door, smiling at her as if he was humouring a small child. 'It will be quicker that way.'

She climbed into the car reluctantly. She didn't want to do this. She had intended just popping into the hospital and asking how the accident victim was. She didn't want to actually visit the man, particularly with a policeman present. She was dragging her feet by the time they got to the injured man's room. The fact that he was awake changed everything, and now she *really* didn't want to do this. She didn't know the man, had never seen him before that night, so what on earth could he want to say to her?

According to Armstrong, he couldn't even remember his name. Short-term amnesia, they called it, brought on by the injuries he'd received. Probably being hit by a car didn't help either, she thought guiltily. But why would he want to talk to her? She didn't know anything about him.

A man in a white jacket hurried past, his head down, and Serena frowned. He looked strangely familiar, but she didn't know any doctors. She was sure she had seen the man recently, but she had no idea where. Still puzzled, she turned her attention to the uniformed policeman sitting outside the door. He was reading a magazine, but he looked up as they approached and then leapt to his feet, trying to stuff the magazine behind the chair. For a moment Serena thought he was going to salute.

'Sir?'

'Any news?'

'No, sir. The man still says he can't remember anything before the incident. He wants to talk to the young lady, though, sir. The one who saved his life.'

'I didn't . . . ' Serena protested, but Armstrong had pushed her inside the door.

She stared at the man in the bed. Was this really the same creature she had found lying in the ditch by the side of the road, his face caked with blood? His hair had appeared dark then, but now she could see it was fair. And he was even younger than she had imagined. Barely out of his teens, she guessed, although it was difficult to see past the bruising and abrasions on his swollen face and the stitches in his head. He smiled painfully at her, and she noticed his teeth were white and even.

Serena walked slowly towards the bed. 'You look much better.'

'Yeah, cleaned up he doesn't look too bad, does he?' Jack Armstrong positioned his body between her and the man in the bed. 'But he's the same person, whoever that is, and for all we know about him, he might be a dangerous lunatic.'

'How can I help?' Serena asked, trying to get round the tall detective. The injured man looked about as dangerous as a sick puppy.

Armstrong practically pushed her into a chair. 'Sit down. You can talk to him from there.'

'I can't remember anything,' the man

in the bed looked at Serena pleadingly. 'I can't remember that night. Only you leaning over me, telling me that you were going to get help. Did I say anything?'

'You said 'phone', and 'left', not much else that I could understand.' She hesitated. The man in the bed was gazing at her pleadingly. She stared back at him. Should she mention the numbers? Yes or no?

'Nothing else.' If she had to make a decision, she'd make it quickly and worry about it later.

'Does that help? Jog your memory at all?' Armstrong asked.

The man tried to shake his head, winced, and shut his eyes.

The detective turned his attention to Serena. 'How about you? Do you remember anything else he said?' When she shook her head, he put his notebook back in his pocket with a sigh. 'If no one can remember anything, we're not going to get far. All this is a bit of a waste of time.'

Serena smiled politely. 'Well, you organised the trip. I didn't ask to come here. I had other plans.'

He held her arm all the way back to the car, more tightly if she tried to wriggle free.

'Am I in custody?' she asked at last.

'No.' He let her go and she rubbed her arm where his fingers had pressed into her flesh.

'Then don't manhandle me.'

He opened the passenger door and waited while she climbed inside, then he bent down until his face was on a level with hers.

'Miss Conti, if I manhandle you, I promise you'll know about it. That was just holding your arm to guide you.' He waited while she wriggled her short skirt down over her thighs. 'I didn't want you tripping over your dress.'

He walked around to the other side of the car and manoeuvred himself awkwardly into the driving seat. 'They should make cars with more leg room.'

Depends on the legs, Serena thought.

Her height of five feet two often meant she had to slide the seat forward before she could reach the pedals.

'I think our victim is lying,' Armstrong said, starting the engine. 'I don't believe in amnesia,'

'Oh, it does exist.' Serena had taken A-level psychology. 'It's not like the tooth fairy.'

'You mean the tooth fairy doesn't exist? Why did no one tell me?' He eased the car into the lunchtime traffic. 'So? What else do you know?'

'Sorry?' Serena answered uneasily.

'Something else. Something you're not telling me, or something you don't think is important.'

When she didn't answer, he laughed softly.

'If there *is* something else, I'll find out.'

When she still didn't answer he said, 'Lunch?'

'Sorry?' she said again.

'Lunch. The stuff you eat. Food. I'm hungry, and as far as I know you

34

haven't eaten since breakfast, so you should be hungry too.' He pulled up outside a McDonalds. 'I find all these long explanations really boring. Do you think you could try and catch on a bit quicker?'

She didn't want to eat with this man. She sat stubbornly in her seat next to him, determined not to move. He climbed out the driver's side, slammed the car door and marched off into the restaurant, not bothering to check whether she was following.

Amazingly, she found herself near to tears. What on earth was the matter with her? She squirmed in her seat, undecided what to do. Whether to follow him or stay where she was. She had made up her mind she didn't like this man right from the start, but finding out he didn't seem to like her either was quite upsetting. Serena was used to being liked. She considered herself a likeable person.

She chewed her bottom lip, looking anxiously out of the car window. Was he going to order a meal for himself and leave her out here to starve? Her stomach rumbled ominously. Just as she had decided she would have to swallow her pride and follow him inside, he came striding back out, carrying two paper sacks. He dumped both on her lap.

'I've got to take you back home, so we'll eat at your place.' He started the car engine, turning his head to grin at her. 'You can make me coffee.'

The smell of the food almost had her drooling, and there was very little point in arguing with the man, he was bound to win. She just hoped Simon hadn't come back unexpectedly. He wouldn't take kindly to a policeman in his home.

'I thought you detectives worked in pairs. How come you're always on your own?'

He turned to look at her. 'Why? Do I make you nervous?'

She shook her head. 'Not at all. And you've answered my question. You're obviously impossible to work with.'

He parked in the car park next to her hire car and waited while she found her door key. Once inside, she opened the door to Simon's apartment and made for the tiny kitchen, opening the bags while she was still moving. Burgers in buns, fries, and a side of onion rings. The smell was sheer heaven. She put two plates and a bottle of ketchup on the counter and tipped the food from the bags. She was about to offer Armstrong a fork, but he was already tucking into his burger after smothering his fries in salt.

'Vinegar?' he asked with his mouth full.

She found the bottle he wanted in a cupboard and handed it to him. Pulling up a stool, she opened her bun and squeezed a generous amount of ketchup on her burger. Squashing the two halves together again, she took a bite and moaned with pleasure. 'Do you live alone?' She couldn't imagine any woman putting up with him for long.

'Mind your own business,' he answered mildly, handing her a paper towel. 'You've got sauce on your chin.' When she looked blank, he translated. 'Ketchup. We'll have to watch this language barrier thing. English is obviously a problem for you.'

'Do you have to work at being rude?' she asked. 'Or does it come naturally?'

'Oh, I think I was probably born with the talent.'

The food was delicious and reminded her of home. Simon wasn't one for fast food. She was mopping up ketchup with her fries when a sudden buzzing sound startled her. Armstrong had placed his phone on the countertop and now it was jiggling about as it vibrated on Simon's shiny black granite. He picked it up and pressed it against his ear. Getting to his feet he moved away from her.

'Good. Send them through to me now.' He glanced at Serena. 'We circulated his finger prints and his description to the other area stations. This might tell us who he is.'

She watched him studying the screen. 'Well?' she asked.

'Ah, yes. Coffee. Black with two sugars for me. Thanks.'

Tight-lipped, she filled the kettle. 'I was asking about your phone call. What did you find out?'

'Nothing, really. Fingerprints not on file. Not in England, anyway. Did he look English to you? He did to me. No accent. One tattoo, badly done. Blood group O Positive. No dental work to speak of. Average height, average build, average bloody everything. Nothing! And if you really believe that amnesia business, you'll believe anything.'

'Can't you trace the tattoo?'

'Our expert says it was probably done abroad, so no, we can't.'

'He could really have lost his memory.' Serena was more doubtful herself now. 'Do you have a neurologist's report?'

'I have a report from just about everybody.' He flicked a finger across the screen. 'Here it is. Post traumatic shock. Post concussional syndrome. Retrograde amnesia. Lying through the teeth. Call it what you like, the man's not talking.' He looked at Serena. 'It also says he suffered a blow to the head that might have caused amnesia. Like being hit by a car.'

'Does it say that?' She tried to grab the phone but he held it out of reach.

'No. This report says it was probably something that happened before you hit him. I was just speculating.'

'Well, how about you go and speculate somewhere else, Mr Armstrong. I have things to do.'

'Me to, but I need my shot of caffeine first. Please may I have a cup of coffee if I promise not to wind you up again?' He gave a regretful little sigh. 'It's just so much fun.'

She poured boiling water into the coffee pot. Anything to get rid of the man. She turned round to find him leaning against the counter, his hands behind his head, studying her.

'What?'

He laughed. 'Just looking. And wondering about your origins. The accent is not very strong, but definitely American, not a trace of Italian, and yet your name is Italian, and you look Italian.'

He took his arms from behind his head and leant forward, bringing his face close to hers. She almost moved away from him, but managed to stop herself. If he was trying to intimidate her, he wasn't going to get away with it. She could feel his breath warm on her face, smell a faint trace of toothpaste mixed with vinegar. She felt a small shiver run through her. He reached out and touched her cheek, and this time she did move away.

'Dark skin and hair, and those eyes . . . ' he paused. 'I remember reading a book once where the heroine was Italian and had eyes 'as dark as sin'. Your eyes are definitely Italian.'

She filled two mugs with coffee and managed to keep her voice almost normal as she answered him. 'I live mainly in the US, but I sometimes come over to England on business.' As an afterthought she added, 'My father was Italian.'

'Was? Is he dead?'

'I don't know.'

He sipped his coffee thoughtfully and then smiled at her. 'This is good. Incidentally, it can be dangerous to keep secrets.' He finished his coffee in silence and then got to his feet. 'Right. Time I was off, then.'

Serena nodded, surprised he hadn't questioned her further. She put the plates in the dishwasher with her breakfast dishes and turned the machine on. 'I'll come down with you to the parking lot. I have to pick up something for Simon in town.'

She grabbed her keys and handbag and followed him to the lift.

He walked her to her car and waited while she slipped into the driving seat. He was about to walk away when she shot out again.

'Someone broke into my car.'

3

Jack Armstrong stood at the window of his shared office on the second floor of the police building and thought about Serena Conti. She was a puzzle, that one. Pretty, if you liked them small and dark. He preferred tall blondes, but Miss Serena Conti of the sinful eyes had got under his skin for some reason — and she was hiding something. Why, he had no idea, but he didn't believe for a minute she had told him everything. Any more than he believed the victim had really lost his memory. They were both lying. But why?

Armstrong shrugged. He didn't believe in wasting time on questions he couldn't answer. Serena Conti's car had been ransacked, but nothing had been taken. Not anything she was telling him about anyway. And the mystery man still wasn't in a fit state to question thoroughly.

Dead ends all round.

He had just started looking at hard copies of the reports for the second time when his telephone rang. He listened for a moment, frowning, and then shrugged back into his jacket. He had only just left the hospital, but now he had been called back urgently. Someone had tried to kill the unidentified man.

The uniformed policeman was still sitting outside the door of the room, his face the colour of the grey hospital walls. He was clutching a polystyrene beaker of what looked like tea, but he hastily shoved the container under his chair when he saw Jack Armstrong approaching.

'I'm sorry, sir. I thought he was a doctor. He looked like a doctor.'

'Start at the beginning, please, officer. I don't have time to listen to gabble.'

'This man in the white coat, who I thought was a doctor, went into the room and came out again, and a few minutes later all the alarms went off. I didn't know what to do so I ran into the room and the patient had something in his mouth. I fished out as much as I could and shouted for a nurse. She called the resuscitation team. He's going to be all right, sir.'

'No thanks to you. You were supposed to be guarding that man. Stopping unauthorised people going in. As if the victim hadn't been through enough already, you let a potential murderer into his room just because the felon was dressed like a doctor.' Armstrong glared at the young constable. 'Get up!'

He waited until the man had climbed shakily to his feet.

'Perhaps if we do away with the chair, you'll stay awake. If you're going to let everyone in a white coat into the room, we could have a queue. Someone wants this man dead, that is already an established fact. You allowed them to have a second go at him. I very much doubt he will survive a third attempt. Do you understand me?'

The man nodded.

Jack Armstrong picked up the chair and moved it several feet down the corridor.

'No chair.'

The constable nodded again, his back stiff as a ramrod.

Armstrong smiled to himself and went in to see the patient, but this time the patient wasn't talking. He had a mask over his face and even more tubes snaking under the bed. A nurse was sitting by his side, watching the machines flashing and bleeping next to her.

She got to her feet when she saw Armstrong, looking worried, but relaxed when he showed her his identification.

'How is he?'

The nurse smiled. 'Alive, thanks to the young man outside. When the alarm went off, he acted straight away. Didn't waste any time, thank goodness. A paper towel had been shoved in the patient's mouth. Without some help he might have choked before we got to him.'

Armstrong worried a back molar with his tongue, staring thoughtfully at the man in the bed. 'I need to speak to him.'

'Impossible. He's been sedated.' The nurse started checking charts, making notes on a pad.'

'I didn't say I wanted to speak to him. I said I need to speak to him. He was conscious when I saw him a little while ago. He must have seen who tried to kill him. I need to talk to him.'

'I'll fetch his doctor,' the nurse said.

They were only prepared to give Armstrong a few minutes, but he hoped that was going to be enough. They took the mask off the patient's face and gave him a shot of something to wake him up.

'Who did it?'

The man peered through half lowered lids. He seemed to recognise Armstrong. 'Don't know what he wanted,' he whispered. 'Can't remember. Told her, that girl . . . '

He coughed, a rasping sound, like a

death rattle, and the doctor moved quickly, slapping the mask back over the man's face, pushing a syringe into his arm.

'Go,' the doctor said, and Jack Armstrong went.

He stood outside the door for a moment, fuming, while the young policeman watched, wondering what awful wrath was about to fall on his head this time.

Armstrong smashed his fist into the palm of his open hand. Stupid girl! Why had she lied? She evidently had information someone was prepared to kill for. What on earth was she playing at? He started down the corridor, then picked up the chair and took it back to the constable.

'Sit if you need to,' he said. 'Just don't go to sleep on the job.'

Armstrong tried to get protection for Serena, but the Chief wasn't buying. No evidence, he said. No evidence that Serena Conti was in any sort of danger. She hadn't asked for protection and, in any case, protection from what? An unknown man who stuffed a paper towel in a patient's mouth? Probably a nut case from the psychiatric ward down the corridor.

Jack Armstrong went home, but he couldn't get little Miss Conti out of his mind. He remembered her sitting at the breakfast bar with sauce on her chin, arguing with him over just about everything. He looked at his watch. It was late, but he had to see her. Find out what she knew that was worth killing for.

The car park in front of her apartment block was badly lit, making shadows move in the corners away from the light. Twice, he thought he heard something, and stood still, waiting. Sometimes you can wait them out, a battle of wills to see who moves first, but this time there was nothing. Even so, he felt a sense of unease, the hairs on the back of his neck telling him all was not right. In the end, he had to leave it. Other than a complete search of the car park, there was nothing he could do.

The lift was slow, working against gravity, the lights flickering on and off. The upstairs corridor was dark as well. Another bulb gone? Thick pile carpets muffled his footsteps and he had trouble finding the right door in the dim light. He hesitated before ringing the bell. What if the boyfriend was at home? Would he be interrupting anything by his late call?

What the hell!

He pushed the bell and listened to the sound reverberating inside the apartment.

★   ★   ★

Serena put down her book with a little tut of annoyance. She had been looking forward to an evening on her own. Simon was staying over at his girlfriend's and wouldn't be home until the morning. She had been curled up on the sofa with a book she had been meaning to read for ages, a glass of white wine beside her, a bag of potato chips on her lap. She looked at her watch. Almost ten o'clock. Too late for a social call, surely.

She turned on the hall light and peered through the spy hole but she couldn't see anything. The hallway outside was unusually dark. She opened the door a couple of inches, then all the way.

'What?' she said.

'Do I get to come in?' He walked past her. 'You should have the chain on. I could have been anyone.'

'I wish you had been,' she said tartly. 'What do you want at this time of night?'

'I need to talk to you. You're not only stupid, you're a liar.

Serena would have laughed if she hadn't been so annoyed. This man was just incredible.

'You can't walk in here and call me names.'

'I just did. As I said before, you're a

liar — and would you mind putting some clothes on.'

Serena looked down at herself. She was wearing a knee length tee shirt and not much else. Her usual night attire.

'I wasn't expecting company.'

'Fine. If you're happy with it.'

'No, wait.' She waved her hands at him, shaking her head at the same time, a gesture Armstrong had come to recognise as uniquely her own, then she opened a door and disappeared inside, reappearing a few seconds later clad in a pink towelling robe. 'Now stop calling me names and tell me what you want.'

He took a deep breath. 'I want you to tell me the truth. Someone tried to kill our accident victim. The man with no name. They nearly succeeded. They wanted the information he says he gave to you.' He took her arm and marched her into the living room. 'So talk, young lady. I'm not going until you do.'

Serena rubbed her arm. 'Someone tried to kill the man in the hospital?'

'What exactly did you not understand about that statement? Someone stuffed a paper towel in the victim's mouth and left him to choke to death.'

Jack Armstrong looked really angry. Stubble made a shadow on his chin, and he looked tired as well as cross. She believed what he said. Someone had tried to kill the accident victim and Detective Inspector Jack Armstrong wasn't going to go until she told him what she knew. The only trouble was, she didn't really know very much, and it probably wasn't worth all the secrecy.

'Are you on duty?' she asked.

He shook his head. 'No. Believe it or not, I came here out of the kindness of my heart.'

Serena picked up her glass of wine. 'Drink?'

'I'm driving, but you have as much as you like. You're not going anywhere, and it might loosen your tongue.'

She took a sip of wine and curled up again on the sofa, her legs tidily tucked up underneath her. Wrapping her robe around her knees, she looked up at him. She wouldn't let him upset her

'Why don't you sit down.' She was surprised when he obediently sat opposite her.

'Well?'

'I don't know much more than I told you. When the man was in the ditch, he mumbled some numbers, but I don't remember what they were.'

Armstrong was quiet for a moment, looking at her, his eyes never leaving her face.

'But you wrote them down.'

She sighed. 'Yes, I wrote them down.' She got up and went into the bedroom, coming back with a slip of paper. Jack Armstrong took it from her.

'Just six numbers? Is that all you've got?'

Serena sat down beside him. 'Yes. Just six numbers. Maybe a phone number?'

He waved the paper at her. 'A phone number isn't worth dying for. Why didn't you tell me before? What was the big secret?'

'Because it might not be a phone number. It might be a bank account number or a safety deposit box number, and you're supposed to keep that sort of thing a secret.' She thought for a minute. 'If there are six numbers, it's not a pin number, so what else has six numbers besides a phone number? I suppose it could be a password for something, like on the Internet.'

'It could be damn near anything. There might have been more than six, but you didn't hear them. You said the victim was mumbling.' He frowned, staring at the paper. 'I suppose he could have remembered something when he was lying in the ditch, but forgotten it later. According to the doctor he had a slow bleed in his head which has now stopped.'

'So you've changed your mind. You think he really did lose his memory.'

'Now I have some medical evidence, yes, it's possible. And since we're baring our souls, are you sure you've told me absolutely everything this time?'

'You mean, am I lying again?'

He turned to look at her and she thought she saw a glimmer of amusement in his eyes.

'Something like that, yes.'

'Well, that's all I've got. All I know. That, and the words I told you about before. Something to do with phones, and left — as opposed to right.' She looked up at him. 'But no one could have known he said anything, because you're the only person I told, so why should I be in any danger?'

'For goodness sake, girl, don't you read the papers?'

'Not that much.' He was making her feel guilty again. She squirmed on her seat. 'Simon gets The Times.'

'You should read the tabloids. A nice little column about your encounter with our victim, and a pretty picture. It makes good reading if you believe a word of it. You evidently saved the poor man's life.'

'I didn't say that,' she protested, colouring. 'And I didn't say anything about what he said to me.'

'No, but you said he spoke to you. That was enough. Dying man's last words to the pretty young American who saved his life, and all that.'

She looked at him aghast. 'Really?'

'Really.'

She thought for a moment. 'It still doesn't make sense. Why try and kill the man if he knows something important? That's stupid.'

'Quite likely. But they've tried twice to get him to talk, without success, and now they think he's passed the information on to you, so they don't really need him any more.'

'So now I'm due for the beating up and the paper towel in the mouth?'

He shook his head. 'You needn't worry about the paper towel. They'll want you alive.'

'Gee, thanks.'

She wasn't going to let him see he'd scared her. That's exactly what he'd come here to do, and she wasn't about to give him the satisfaction. She got to her feet and walked over to the window, lifting the blind to look down on the car park two levels below. A man was standing in a dim corner. She watched the glow of his cigarette. Not exactly a threat. She couldn't allow herself to be scared by every shadow. This was a quiet country town in England, not downtown New York. She let the blind drop.

'So, what do you suggest I do? Lock myself in the apartment?'

'Just watch your back. Be aware. Tell the boyfriend and get him to watch out for you.'

Tell Simon? That was a joke. Her dear half-brother was more concerned with his reputation than with her life. If she got beaten up, he'd worry about how it would affect his image in the City. Perhaps it was time she told Jack Armstrong what her relationship to Simon really was.

'Listen!'

Armstrong held up his hand, silencing her, and Serena froze. For a moment she couldn't hear anything. Only the usual noises from the block of apartments. Double glazing kept out the street sounds. Only this time, there *was* something. Her ears pricked. Someone outside the front door. A scraping sound, then a thump, then the scraping sound again. Someone trying to break in?

The short hairs on the back of her neck were standing on end, and her arms had goose bumps. Now she really was frightened. She looked at Jack Armstrong but he shook his head, silently shushing her. She watched him move out of the room and start to creep down the hallway. What did he intend to do? He was dressed in jeans and a shirt. No weapon. English cops didn't carry guns. Serena kept close behind him.

As Armstrong reached the front door it opened inwards, nearly hitting him in the face. He jumped back, grabbing Serena with one arm and pushing her behind him to protect her. She let out a little squeak of fear as the dark shape on the threshold straightened up and stared at them.

4

Simon had been bending down to pick up his overnight case. Now he faced them uncertainly, the light from inside partially blinding him.

'Serena? The hall light's blown. I couldn't find the keyhole. Didn't want to ring the bell in case you were in bed.' He stared at Armstrong. 'Who's this?'

Serena untangled herself from the policeman. He still had his arm round her and she was still clutching his shirt. She moved away, re-tying the cord round her robe and running a hand through her hair.

'You startled us. We thought you were trying to break it. Why aren't you in London?'

Simon pushed past them. 'I don't think I should have to explain my actions in front of a complete stranger.' He threw his overnight bag onto a chair and looked at Serena accusingly. 'Next time you entertain someone while I'm away, I'd appreciate being informed.'

'I'm sorry, sir,' Armstrong said easily. 'I'm Detective Inspector Armstrong from the local police station. I just called round to let Miss Conti know that the man she assisted has been attacked in his hospital room. I thought she might have some additional information that could help us. Sorry for the intrusion at this time of night.' He gave Serena a mock salute. 'Put the chain on the door, Miss Conti.'

Before Serena could say anything, he had gone, closing the front door gently behind him.

Simon still looked furious. 'If that man really is a policeman, he should know better. And so should you. You seem to forget I have neighbours, and this is not the sort of place where you entertain men in your nightwear.' Serena was about to say something, but Simon held up his hand like a conductor at the Albert Hall. 'I'm tired,

Serena. We'll talk about this in the morning.'

Effectively dismissed, although she would have liked a hot drink before she went to bed, Serena walked out of the room and closed the door behind her. Once in her bedroom she walked to the window, hoping she might see Jack Armstrong driving away, but he had already gone. There were no men lurking under streetlights and no new cars in the car park, but she was too wound up to go to sleep. Why did Simon have to be such a pretentious prat? Even if she was only his half-sister, they had the same mother. Perhaps that was the problem. Simon took after their mother.

Smiling to herself, Serena climbed into bed. She had to admit she felt safer with Simon back home. He might not be any good with his fists, but he could probably talk an attacker to death. That bought her thoughts back to Jack Armstrong. The man might not carry a gun, but she had felt safer in his arms than with a squad of gun-toting sheriffs guarding her back.

She awoke with the sun shining in her eyes and was about to leap out of bed when she remembered it was Sunday. The events of the previous day seemed slightly ridiculous. She was a promotions manager in England on a job. No one was trying to kill her. Whatever Jack Armstrong might think, that was just plain silly. She got out of bed and opened the window. The traffic was light, but it was still there. People going about their Sunday morning business; picking up the Sunday paper, going to church, taking the dog for a walk. Mundane things people did on a sunny day in a small town.

As Simon seemed to find her robe unsettling, she had a quick shower and dressed in jeans and a t-shirt before she braved him in the kitchen. He was sitting at the breakfast bar eating toast and agonising over the Sunday Times crossword. He pushed the coffee pot towards her.

'Sorry about last night, but you shouldn't allow anybody in when you're dressed for bed, even a policeman.'

'So, what would you suggest? If I'd refused he'd probably have dragged me off to the police station.'

Simon didn't look up from his crossword. 'They don't do that sort of thing in this country. That's something you will have to get used to, Serena. We do things differently in England.' He looked up as she poured the coffee. 'I still don't understand how you saw a man in a ditch on a dark country lane.'

Serena took a breath. Time for a confession? She didn't think so. She preferred to remain a hero — at least in Simon's eyes.

'I was driving slowly because the lane was narrow and I didn't want to finish up in the ditch myself.' All true. 'And I just caught a glimpse of the injured man in my headlights.' Also true. She felt quite pleased with herself. She didn't like telling lies.

'What's all this about him getting

attacked at the hospital?'

'I've no idea.' The truth was beginning to get harder. 'The staff at the hospital think it was someone on a walkabout from the psychiatric wing.'

Simon looked horrified. 'Surely that can't happen?'

Serena patted him on the arm. 'It obviously does in this country. Like you said, they do things differently over here.'

After breakfast, Simon went off to play his usual round of golf and Serena tried to decide what to do with herself. She had been looking forward to a few weeks away from her mother, but now she was on her own, she was at a loss as to how to fill her day. The weather wasn't anything special; a grey day with damp in the air. Not warm enough to go out without a jacket. She had thought she understood the English weather, and she had assumed May would be warm in the south. Now she was finding she had a suitcase full of unsuitable clothes. Thank goodness her job demanded a business suit most of the time.

Pulling on a denim jacket to match her jeans, she let herself out of the apartment and headed for her car. The guy she had hit looked like a student to her, and she wondered if Jack Armstrong was checking out the university. Norbridge was a university town, and whenever she stayed with her brother half the population seemed to be students.

She thought of calling in at the police station, but doubted Armstrong would be there on a Sunday. The man must take some time off. So, instead, she took the road that led to the hospital. She might be able to jog the young man's memory if she reminded him about the numbers.

There was a different policeman outside the door, but he agreed to let her in when she told him who she was and produced ID in the form of her passport. He had heard about her, he said, and what she had done.

'Good job you stopped on that lane, miss. Lot's of others would have just driven on.'

She didn't tell the nice policeman how close she had come to doing just that. Or how much she wished she had.

She was escorted into the room by a nurse. 'He's asleep, I'm afraid,' the woman told Serena apologetically. 'We're keeping him lightly sedated. It will give his brain time to settle down. It had a bit of a trauma and it needs to rest. You can talk to him, though. Just having someone in the room can help the healing process.'

Serena pulled up a chair beside the bed and sat down. The room was basic, but spotlessly clean and quite large. There was a washbasin in the corner, and when she tried another door she found it led to a shower and toilet. A private room with an ensuite. The NHS wasn't so bad, after all.

She sat with her Mr Nobody for half an hour, talking to him now and again but getting no response, and then she told the policeman outside that she was leaving. Simon was right, she wasn't doing any good by getting involved, even if she did still feel responsible for the man she had hit. Everyone kept telling her it wasn't her fault, and she had done the right thing, but she still felt guilty. He must have believed the words he whispered to her were important, and she wished she had listened more carefully. Now he couldn't tell her anything, not even his name.

As she left the room she remembered the man she had seen the day before. The doctor she thought she recognised. It annoyed her when she couldn't remember where she had previously seen a face. She was good with faces. She was unlocking her car in the hospital car park when she remembered exactly where she had seen the man.

Standing quite still, she closed her eyes, feeling an icy finger of fear travel down her spine. She had to see Jack Armstrong, and if he wasn't at the station house she would have to find him somehow. This couldn't be left another day. Besides, next week she had a mountain of work to get through, and she wouldn't be able to work at all with this on her mind.

The man behind the desk at the police station treated her insistence with mild contempt.

'Can't give out phone numbers to all and sundry. Particularly the phone number of a Detective Inspector. More than my job's worth.'

'Can you phone him for me, then, please. Tell him it's urgent.'

'It's a Sunday. More than . . . '

'I know,' Serena said impatiently, 'more than your job's worth. Listen, I have important information about the man who was attacked in hospital yesterday. I think I know who tried to kill him.'

'Our accident victim? It was some nutter from the psych ward.'

'No, it wasn't!' Serena flapped her hands. 'It was a policeman.'

The man behind the desk frowned.

'You want to be careful, making accusations like that. It could get you into trouble.'

Serena shook her head. 'Not a real policeman. He was dressed like a doctor the last time I saw him. Oh, for goodness sake! This is really important. If you can't help me, find someone who can.'

Disgruntled, the man picked up a phone. Five minutes later a woman dressed casually in tight black jeans and a low-cut red top appeared through a door and walked towards Serena. Her hair was almost as red as her top, pulled back into a ponytail. Gold hoop earrings almost touched her shoulders.

'My name's Nina Ford. You asked for Jack Armstrong? He's not in today but I usually work with him. I understand you have information about a police-man posing as a doctor?'

The woman looked as sceptical as the man behind the counter, and Serena could understand why.

'I didn't explain very well,' she said.

'Do you know about the man who can't remember who he is? The one who was attacked yesterday in his hospital room? I think I may know something about the person who attacked him.'

The woman took her arm. 'Let's go into one of the interview rooms. I've been off for a couple of days, so I don't have first-hand information on this, but I can get hold of the file.' She led Serena into a sparsely furnished room with a table and two chairs. 'Have a seat.'

Serena sat awkwardly on the edge of one of the chairs. Don't get involved, she reminded herself, and here she was, causing mayhem in a police station. A uniformed policewoman came in with a file and put it on the table. Nina Ford opened the file and looked up at Serena expectantly.

'It may be nothing, but I saw a man who said he was a policeman, and then I saw him again at the hospital dressed like a doctor, and that was just before someone tried to kill the man I found in a ditch.'

The woman blinked, trying very hard not to look completely confused. 'How about you pretend I don't know anything at all and start from the beginning.' She listened to Serena without a word and then pulled a phone from pocket of her jeans. 'Jack? I think you need to come in.'

Serena had expected him to look annoyed, but he didn't. He walked into the room and gave her a quizzical smile before parking his bottom on the table. That made him a good head and shoulders above both of them, which was obviously his intention.

'So? What have you remembered this time, Miss Conti? It must be fun to hold a few things back. Keeps the excitement going.'

She felt the familiar hatred coming on. 'I really have only just remembered, and I'm not trying to hold anything back.' She felt like a child begging forgiveness for an untruth.

'When I was waiting for the ambulance to arrive, two men turned up in a car. They said they were police detectives and offered to take the injured man to hospital, but I had already called an ambulance, so I said no thanks and they drove off. A proper police car followed the ambulance and I gave them my name and address and told them everything I've just told you. Then I saw a doctor at the hospital yesterday and thought I recognised him. I've only just remembered why he looked familiar. He was one of the two men in the car.'

'A police detective?' Nina Ford said in disbelief.

'I don't think he was.' Serena looked at Armstrong. 'I don't think the man in the hospital was a doctor, either.'

'Would you recognise the man you saw in the hospital again?'

'Possibly. I didn't recognise him straight away because of the white coat. It might depend on what he's wearing.'

The woman sighed. 'People always remember clothes before faces. Put someone in a bright red coat, and that's all the witness ever remembers.'

'How about the car?'

'What car?'

He rolled his eyes. 'The car the two men were in when they stopped at the accident scene. No other car will do, because that's the one I'm interested in right this moment.'

'Something big and square. It was dark,' she told him grumpily.

'Think.'

She closed her eyes. 'Possibly an SUV of some sort. It stopped with the passenger door towards me and I remember the man stepping down out of it.'

'SUV?' Nina asked.

'It's an American abbreviation for Sports Utility Vehicle. Usually a four-wheel drive vehicle.' He turned his attention back to Serena. 'Something like a Range Rover, Miss Conti, or something smaller?'

The car had been in silhouette, a dark blob on the road. She shook her head, frowning. 'More rounded than a

Jeep and smaller than a Hummer. That's the best I can do.'

'Better than nothing. What exactly did they say to you? Close your eyes again and visualise the scene. The car stops, the passenger door is nearest to you. Then what happens?'

'One of them gets out. Slowly.' Her eyes popped open. 'He said something strange. He said something like, 'There's a woman with him'. I didn't think anything of it at the time, but it was odd.'

Jack shot a look at Nina. 'So they were looking for him. Maybe they didn't push him out of the car. Maybe he jumped and they came back to find him. Difficult to turn round on a narrow lane in the dark. By the time they got back, he had company.'

'If he jumped, that would explain his injuries. Hang on, I've got his hospital report here.' She flipped the pages of the file. 'Apart from a blow to the head, the rest are impact injuries. Not necessarily a beating. Jumping out of a car moving at 30 to 40 miles an hour would have the same effect. And he might have crawled into the ditch to hide.'

'Now were getting somewhere.' Jack grinned at Serena. 'See? You can be helpful when you try. Now I have an idea what happened, I might be able to get through to him.' He turned to Nina. 'When are they taking our victim off his meds? I need to talk to him again.'

Nina shut the file. 'I've no idea. Do you want me to phone the hospital now, or wait until tomorrow?'

'Wait until tomorrow. He's not going anywhere, and if Miss Conti can come up with a decent description for one of the men, we'll do an identikit picture and I'll show him that. If he's really lost his memory, a picture might help, and if he hasn't, it could scare him into a confession.'

'Confession!' Serena said incredulously. 'What's he supposed to have done?'

'He must have done something to make him want to jump from a moving car. It's not a particularly popular pastime. You're likely to get hurt.'

'You don't know he did that. You're just speculating again.'

Jack Armstrong got to his feet. 'Yes, and I do it exceedingly well. I have an honours degree in speculation. Now, I suggest you go home and come back tomorrow morning to give us a detailed description of the man you saw.' He took a business card from his pocket and handed it to her. 'And if you remember anything else, perhaps you could phone me. It's nice to be kept informed.'

There was no point in trying to help, Serena thought, as she drove back to Simon's apartment. All it did was get her into trouble. Simon didn't want her living with him, her mother was phoning her every five minutes, and now a police detective was being really nasty to her for no reason at all. She needed to get her British client signed up so she could go back to Sacramento.

She parked her car outside the apartment and looked at her watch. It was past lunchtime and there was probably nothing in the refrigerator to eat. Simon would stay at the golf club for lunch and she didn't fancy eating out on her own. She had been looking forward to visiting England — she had even been looking forward to seeing Simon again — but now she was beginning to think this had been a really bad idea.

She took her door key out of her bag and opened the door with a little sigh.

To be faced with utter chaos.

Every drawer had been upended and every book from the floor to ceiling bookcase lay on the floor. Simon's CD collection was scattered haphazardly around the room and some of the cases had come open, silver discs glinting like forgotten Christmas tree decorations. Through the open door she could see the kitchen in much the same state, with every cupboard door open and every drawer emptied. Cereal packets had been ripped open, tins lay with their lids missing, and instant coffee granules stuck to broken glass.

She ran from room to room making senseless little noises. The bedrooms were the same — the beds stripped and drawers emptied. Even her shoes had been taken from the closet and thrown around the room.

She stood still then, her hands covering her face, with no idea what to do next.

5

Jack Armstrong decided it wasn't worth going home. He might as well stay in his office and search for the car Serena Conti had identified as an SUV. The thought of two bogus policemen irritated him. It seemed anyone could pose as a plain-clothes detective and get away with it. But Serena Conti had been suspicious. She hadn't let the men take the victim away, she had waited for the ambulance. He smiled to himself. Quite bright, that one — but argumentative as hell. He wasn't quite sure why, but she definitely brought out the worst in him. He wasn't usually that rude to anyone, particularly a woman as attractive as Miss Conti.

He had just started looking through the file when his mobile phone began its distinctive ring tone. Armstrong frowned. Conti had barely had time to get back to her boyfriend's flat and she was already calling him. Perhaps he really was irresistible. He punched the answer button and waited.

'Jack?' Her voice sounded strange. 'I didn't know who else to call. Can you come over here, please? Someone's been in the apartment. It's a mess.'

He stood up, almost knocking the chair over. 'Are they still there?'

'No. But it's a real mess. Simon will be livid.'

'I'm on my way.'

He cursed Simon as he ran to his car. Serena didn't look the type to live with someone who scared her. Too frightened to tell him his flat had been broken into because . . . because what? Because he might hurt her?'

The mere thought had Jack pushing his foot to the floor. He had a light on the back seat but he didn't have time to put it on the roof. He realised he should have brought Nina with him, but the thought had never crossed his mind. He heard the catch in Serena

Conti's voice when she called him by his first name, and he needed to get to her as fast as possible.

The traffic was light, which was good because he knew he wasn't driving very well. He stopped in the car park with a scatter of gravel and hurried towards the door into the building. He should have stopped to look around outside. The villains might still be in the vicinity. He knew he was behaving like an idiot and slowed his pace as he walked along the carpeted corridor. He wasn't going to do anyone any good if he left his brain behind. Her door was slightly open, and he held his breath, almost afraid to go inside.

She was sitting on one of the black leather sofas, staring at the destruction in the room, and as his eyes took in the shambles he realised why she might be worried about the wrath of Simon. She was right. The place was a mess.

'Serena?' He couldn't call her Miss Conti when she was crying. He squatted in front of her. 'Listen to me.

If anything's broken or missing, it's just things. No one is hurt, and things can be repaired or replaced. So stop crying and tell me what happened. Did you find it like this?'

She nodded, not looking at him.

'Have you moved anything, tried to tidy up at all?'

Now she looked at him. The tears had left streaks down her cheeks and her mascara had run. 'Does it look as if I've tidied up? I was going to start, but I thought I might disturb the evidence or something. Maybe they left finger-prints. I called you because I didn't fancy a couple of big men in uniform tramping round the place. It's in enough of a mess as it is.'

He almost smiled. 'It is that. You got any alcohol in the place?'

She managed a weak smile. 'I'll have a look, but they might have broken the bottles. They broke most everything else.'

'I'll get it. Just tell me where.'

He found the wine rack in the

kitchen, the bottles safe and sound. Serena's visitors had only broken things where something might be hidden. Something small. Clear glass had been left intact, pictures were still on the walls, the TV probably still worked, and the bottle of brandy he found on the work surface was still in one piece.

He found two shot glasses and poured generous portions. He handed her a glass. 'I'm not on duty, and if I go over the limit I'll have to stay the night.'

She smiled again. 'Another thing Simon wouldn't like. Sorry about the meltdown. I don't usually cry.'

'If this had been my place, I might have shed a few tears, but I think it looks worse than it actually is. Whoever did this isn't your run-of-the-mill vandal. They were looking for something specific, something they think you've got.' He frowned at her. 'If you're hiding something, Serena, you need to tell me.'

'I'm not hiding anything, Jack,' she said, emphasising his first name. 'I promise I would tell you if I was. This has scared the hell out of me, not just because it's Simon's apartment, but because I really don't know what they want, or what they're looking for.'

'Not a piece of paper with some numbers on it, that's for sure. If that had been what they wanted, they'd have come while you were at home and forced you to tell them.'

She shivered. 'I wouldn't have needed much forcing.'

'Exactly. Finish your drink and you can tell me if anything's missing.'

He wanted to get her moving. Stop her thinking about what might have happened if she *had* still been at home. And he was beginning to wonder if she really was the target. What if this had nothing to do with the injured man and was all to do with the boyfriend. Something he had that someone else wanted. He'd checked on Simon, and the man worked for a legal firm in the City. He was a solicitor, hardly likely to be handling a high-profile case, but you could never tell.

'How does your long-range romance work?' he asked as he followed her from room to room.

'Pardon?' She gave him a distracted look. 'What long-range romance?'

'You and this Simon.' He picked up an unbroken glass by the base and put it on one side, ready for bagging. Any shiny object that had obviously been moved might still have fingerprints on it, but he was betting they'd worn gloves.

'Simon is my brother. My half-brother, if you must know. He kindly lets me stay here when I'm in England.' She sighed. 'He hates publicity, so first of all I get my name in the paper, and now I'm responsible for someone trashing his home.'

She looked as if she might cry again but he had trouble keeping the relief out of his voice when he said, 'Your brother? I thought he was your boyfriend.'

'I know you did.' He got another

damp smile. 'Although, actually, it's none of your business. Besides, I might have a whole posse of boyfriends back home in Sacramento.'

'But you don't, do you?' It was his turn to sigh. 'And that could be a problem.'

She stopped moving and turned to look at him, wide-eyed. 'Why?'

He knew he was treading on quicksand, but he couldn't stop himself. 'Because I'm not supposed to get involved with anyone connected to a police investigation.'

Her eyes were enormous now. 'But you're not involved with me.'

'I know.' He moved closer to her. 'But that was partly because I thought you were already living with someone else, and now I know you're not.' He rested his hands on her upper arms and felt her tremble. It could have been from fear or desire, he had no way of knowing, but she didn't move away.

'I *am* living with someone else. My brother. And I don't like you, Jack

Armstrong. You're rude and arrogant. Not my type at all.'

'I'm not asking you to like me. Sometimes a little hostility adds to the heat.'

Now she did move away, rubbing her arms where he had held her. 'I don't think there is anything missing, but this is not my apartment and I don't make a habit of searching through Simon's belongings, so something could have been taken. You need to talk to him.'

'Indeed I do. But I think you feel the heat as well, Miss Conti, so we shall both have to be very careful.'

★ ★ ★

She tried not to let him see how much he really disturbed her. She should never have told him Simon was her brother. Thinking Simon was her boyfriend had kept him at arms length, and that is exactly where she intended keeping him in the future. She didn't want involvement, didn't have time for involvement, particularly with someone like Jack Armstrong. She had been telling the truth, she really didn't like him. The trouble was, she fancied him like mad, and if he ever found out it would make her time in England extremely difficult.

'Can I start clearing up?' Now Armstrong was back over the other side of the room she had her faculties back. 'I know I'll have to tell Simon, but it won't be so bad if the place is clean and tidy. He can go through everything when he gets home and work out if anything is missing.'

'You want me to go?'

No, she didn't, but while he was here in the room with her she couldn't think straight; and it wouldn't be a good idea for Simon to find him still here when he got home. She looked round the room again and sighed. She was never going to get the place tidy on her own.

'No,' she told him reluctantly. 'I don't want you to go. I want you to help me clear up. I called you because I was desperate, but Simon may not want to involve the police. If I tell him it was a case of random vandalism — he'll go along with that. He doesn't want his name in the papers.'

'I don't think you can keep this quiet, Serena. But I'm not here on official duty, and I suppose, technically, it's not a robbery if nothing's missing.' He looked round the room. 'Where do you want me to start?'

What she really wanted to do was give him a big hug, but that would probably delay the clearing up process.

It took them an hour. The detective insisted on wielding the vacuum cleaner and looked as if he was actually enjoying it. They didn't talk much. Jack kept saying things like, 'Where does this go?' and mostly she had no idea. The problem of when to tell Simon would never arise, she realised. He would know as soon as he walked in the door. She wished she had paid more attention to where everything had originally been placed. The little bronze mermaid didn't look right on the coffee table, but she couldn't remember where it had been before the break-in. Tidied up and vacuumed to within an inch of its life, the apartment looked almost normal, and that was the best they could do.

'I don't like leaving you here on your own.'

She looked at him worriedly. 'You think they'll come back?'

He shook his head. 'No, actually I don't. They gave the place a pretty thorough going over and whatever they were looking for isn't here — unless they found it. Either way, they won't come back. There's no point.'

'And Simon will be home in about an hour,' she said. 'So I'll be fine.'

'Do you want me to stay until Simon gets back?'

She shook her head. 'No, please don't. It will make things worse. My brother is very protective. That's why he doesn't like you.'

'My popularity rating is not too good at the moment, is it? Don't I get

Brownie points for helping you clear up?'

She held the door open for him. 'Thank you for helping, Jack. I do appreciate it.'

'I'm glad about that.' Before she knew what was happening, he had placed a hand on either side of her head, holding it still, and dropped a light kiss on her lips. 'I'll see you tomorrow.'

Her lips were still tingling some time after he had left the building. Not knowing whether to be angry or amused, she poured herself another brandy and waited for Simon to come home.

When he eventually walked into the room it took a few moments before he noticed anything was wrong, and for that she was grateful to Jack Armstrong.

'What on earth have you been doing, Serena. You shouldn't move things around without asking.' He picked up the little mermaid and put her back on the windowsill. His eyes roved the room and settled on the bookcase. 'What was wrong with the way my books were arranged, for goodness sake?'

'Nothing's wrong with your book arrangement.' For some reason she started to cry again. 'We had a break-in. Someone burglarised the apartment. I don't know if they took anything, but they messed the place up pretty good.' She was slipping back into the Americanisms he hated, and tried to stop herself. 'I'm really sorry, Simon.'

Much to her surprise, he put his arm round her. 'Are you all right? Did anyone hurt you?'

'No.' She snuffled into his shirtfront. 'I was out. I came back to it. We've tidied up the best we could, but a few things were broken. Jack Armstrong wants you to let him know if anything has been taken.'

'You called the police?'

He was looking horrified and she moved away from him, shaking her head. 'No. I called Jack because I trust him.' Did she really believe that? 'He wasn't on duty, and he won't report this unless you want him to. If nothing's been taken there's no need. The place was a mess, but we cleared up.'

Simon ran both hands through his thinning hair. 'Why would anyone want to break in here? It must have been as risky as hell to do it in broad daylight.' He looked round the room and then opened a drawer in the sideboard. He reached in to the back of the drawer and turned round flourishing a wad of banknotes.

'I keep a couple of hundred pounds in here in case I need some ready cash. Why didn't they take it?'

'I don't know. Jack thinks they were looking for something specific. Were you hiding something, Simon? Something valuable.'

'Good heavens, no! Of course not. Apart from a bit of ready cash, what would I have to hide?' He took a breath. 'Does this have anything to do with the man you found injured? I really can't cope with this, Serena.

Bradley and Partners is cutting back. They're looking for the slightest excuse . . . '

'You mean you might lose your job? Oh, Simon, I'm so sorry.'

He slumped back on to the sofa. 'So it does have something to do with the man in the ditch.'

'I don't know. I can't imagine how it could, but I don't know for sure. Jack said he's not going to tell anyone about the break-in, so we can keep this quiet if that's what you want.'

He looked defeated. 'I just want to get back to normal.'

Serena sat down beside him. 'It's my fault. I should move out. I can't leave England for another few weeks, but I can find somewhere else to stay.'

'I'm not kicking you out.' He picked up her empty glass. 'Did you finish all my brandy, or is there enough for another couple of shots?'

She smiled at him. 'Thank you for being so nice about all this.'

'I don't have much option.'

By the time Serena had finished her

second drink she was feeling quite light-headed. Simon worked methodically, noting the breakages — in case he wanted to make an insurance claim — and putting everything back in its proper place as he went along. Serena watched with admiration. That was a gene she hadn't inherited. She smiled. He might be a pain in the ass, but she'd miss him when she went back home.

She was getting ready for bed when Jack Armstrong called on her mobile.

'How did big brother take the news? Anything missing from the flat?'

'Nothing's been taken and Simon's been really good about everything. I think this must have been a random break-in, whoever it was got interrupted and that's why they left empty-handed.'

'You think what you like. Whatever makes you happy. I've got my own ideas. Also, a bit of good news. We've had a missing persons report and it looks like it might be your accident victim.'

'Mr Nobody? Oh, that's wonderful! I

thought someone must be missing him by now. When can I see him?'

'You can't. Not until we know what's going on.'

She kicked off her slippers and bounced on the bed. 'You can't cut me out now. I need to know what's going on as well. Someone burgled Simon's flat.'

'You were the one who said the break-in wasn't connected, so until you hear from me, stay away from the victim.'

She was getting used to his bossiness. 'I was going to phone you anyway. I remembered after you left that I have an appointment in London tomorrow, so I won't be able to do the face recognition thing. I can probably spare some time the next day.'

'Don't put yourself out. We probably won't need you, anyway, now our man's been identified.'

The phone went dead in her hand. She cursed mildly. She had so many questions to ask she felt she might burst. Who had made the report to the police? Family, friends? And would Mr Nobody recognise anyone if they turned up at his bedside? The hospital was dead set on keeping him sedated, so Jack might have to wait for his answers as well.

She wandered over to the window and stared out at the empty street. A spark, like a firefly, glittered briefly in a shady corner and she saw the shadow of a man. Whoever it was had just stubbed his cigarette out on someone's gatepost. Serena pressed her nose against the glass. Was it the same man as last night? The shadow moved and was gone, blending in to the dark. She sighed, and climbed in to bed.

That was another question that would have to wait for an answer.

6

Serena had an appointment in London the next day and knew she wouldn't be back until early afternoon, but the trains were delayed and she didn't get back to the apartment until late evening. Simon was already home. He looked tired, she thought.

'Have you eaten?'

He shook his head. 'I only got back half an hour ago.'

'Do you want to eat out or shall I order something in?'

'There's pasta in the freezer and salad in the fridge. I'll throw something together'

She tossed her laptop case on the sofa and hung her jacket behind the door. 'No, I'll do it. Do you want me to get you a drink?'

He blinked at her wearily. 'You've already said sorry, Serena. No need to go overboard — but a glass of red would be nice. Open a new bottle.'

The pasta only took a few minutes and by the time it was ready Simon had set the table. 'Mother phoned just before you got in,' he said. 'She told me you're avoiding her.'

'She's driving me mad. She won't sell the house, and she can't afford to live there on her own. I'd love to have my own place, but I can't leave her. Since she lost her position with Barnett Enterprises she's gotten worse.'

'She shouldn't have left Dad. He was never the same after that. I was only ten, but I remember how devastated he was.'

'From what I heard, your father kicked Mother out.'

Simon spooned pasta onto his plate with more energy than was necessary. 'She was pregnant with another man's baby, Serena. What did you expect him to do?'

Serena shook her head. 'I don't know. But it wasn't my fault, and I got left with no father at all. She didn't bother to tell my father she was pregnant.'

'She probably couldn't remember who he was.'

'She knew who he was. She gave me his name.'

For some reason her mother had insisted the name Conti was put on her certificate of birth, rather than Prescott. Wishful thinking, maybe. Hoping he would come back.

Simon reached across the table and touched Serena's hand. 'Sorry, that was uncalled for. I love Mother, but I'm not sorry she lives across the other side of the Atlantic. Perhaps I should have gone with her, but Dad wanted me to stay, and all my friends were here.'

'I don't blame you, Simon. Not for one minute. She was the one who broke up the family. I would have loved a brother around when I was growing up, but she didn't tell me about you until I was five.'

He smiled. 'And at fifteen the last thing I wanted was a baby sister.'

She took his empty plate. 'But we got together in the end.'

'Only because you need a place to crash when you're in England.' He held up his hand. 'Only joking. You know you're very welcome, but try and stay out of trouble while you're here, will you? I don't need the extra hassle at the moment.'

'How is work?'

He shrugged. 'No one knew I had a sister until yesterday. Now they can't wait to meet you.'

She laughed. 'I promise I won't introduce myself to your work colleagues, not if you'd rather keep me a secret, and I don't really blame you. A mad mother, and a sister on a police register — probably not much of an asset. Some good news. I think the Mr Nobody thing may be over. Someone's reported him missing.'

★　★　★

The young man peered at Jack Armstrong's ID before fully opening the door. He started to hold out his hand and then changed his mind.

'I'm Mike Astley,' he said nervously. 'Come in. It's a bit of a mess, I'm afraid.'

It was. Jack stood in the middle of a room barely big enough for a cluttered sofa. The only other piece of furniture was a coffee table holding a laptop computer and a pile of books. An open door led off to a kitchen area with a sink full of dirty dishes, the small dining table covered in more books. He could see laundry piled on top of a loaded washing machine and caught himself wondering what the bedrooms must look like. After searching for somewhere to sit down he decided to remain standing.

'I need to ask you a few questions, Mr Astley.'

Astley sat on the arm of the sofa. 'When I phoned the police station they told me Liam's in hospital. When can I see him?'

'Maybe tomorrow. He had a serious

head wound which caused a few problems. He's lost a lot of his memory so he may not know you. I need to confirm what you told the officer when you phoned in.' Jack took out his notebook and turned the pages. 'Your flat-mate has been missing for three days; he has fair hair, a light complexion, and a tattoo on his left arm. An eagle with a missing claw. Is that correct?'

'Yeah. Liam had the tattoo done when he was . . . when he'd had a bit too much to drink. The guy who did it wasn't very good. The tattoo looks more like a sparrow than an eagle — and its got three toes on one foot and two on the other. Liam said he didn't notice until the next morning and it was hurting like hell by then, so there was no way he was going back for the other toe.'

Jack managed to keep his face expressionless. 'It certainly sounds as if our unidentified man is your flat-mate. Has he been in any trouble recently?

Upset someone enough for them to put him in hospital? He was pretty badly beaten before he ended up in the ditch.'

'Some girl found him, didn't she? I saw it in the paper, and that's when I began to worry about Liam. At first I thought he'd scored big time and stayed the night with some bird. But then he didn't turn up for lectures, either, so I got a bit worried. Even if he was hung over he would've managed to get to some of the classes. He takes uni seriously.'

'You didn't answer my question.'

'Oh? No, sorry. No one was out to get him or anything. Not as far as I know, anyway.'

'And as far as you know he wasn't keeping anything here that someone might be looking for? Drugs, money, anything valuable?'

When Astley shook his head, Jack thought for a moment. 'I presume your friend had a bank account. Do you know his account number?' Another shake. 'Or anything else that might need six numbers to gain access, maybe something that needs a password?'

'Everything needs a password, but I don't know any of Liam's.'

'And you haven't come across anything unusual in the flat? Something that wasn't there before?'

Michael Astley rubbed his nose. 'No, not really. The place looked fine when I came home that day . . . only . . . '

'Only . . . ?' Jack prompted.

'Only I took my shoes off because my feet were hot — and the carpet was wet. I thought spilt beer, something like that, you know? But when the wet patch dried it left a sort of brown stain. Beer doesn't do that.'

'No, beer doesn't. Where is this stain?'

The stain was beside the coffee table, which was a heavy oak affair obviously bought to outlast any number of students. It had rounded corners exactly the right shape to cause a blunt-trauma wound to the head. The patch on the floor was about the size of a dinner plate. Jack found more brown stains by the door. He was already 100% sure the marks were blood, and that was something that would be reasonably easy to confirm.

'Nothing else out of place when you came in that evening?'

Astley waved an arm to encompass the room. 'I probably wouldn't notice.'

'I'd like to have a look at his bedroom — and yours if you don't mind.'

Jack did a quick search of the bedrooms, anything more thorough would need a warrant, and promised to get Michael in to see his friend the next morning. He was eager to get a positive ID, and he had a nasty feeling that while the villains were still on the loose, Serena Conti was still in danger. He had no idea why she was in danger, but he worried about her. He had no idea why he worried about her, either.

* * *

Serena got up early and shifted her morning appointment to the afternoon. Whatever Jack Armstrong said over the phone, he had no authority to tell her what to do. If she wanted to call in at the hospital to check on a friend, that was her business.

An enquiry at reception told her Mr Nobody was still in a coma. The girl looked up from her computer screen with a smile. 'The policeman brought someone with him to see the patient, so we may know who he is soon. It will be nice to call the poor man by his name.'

'What do you call him at the moment?' Serena asked curiously. Anything was probably better than Mr Nobody.

The girl looked up and down the corridor before she answered. 'Cutie Pie.' She blushed pink. 'One of the nurses said how cute he was and it kind of stuck. Not to his face, of course,' she added hastily, 'or when the doctors are around.'

Much better than Mr Nobody,

Serena thought, as she made her way to the lift. She didn't want to meet Jack Armstrong because he would stop her going into the room, so she thought it might be a good idea to check the coast was clear. She walked slowly along the corridor, smiling at passing nurses and doctors, until she got to the policeman guarding the door to the room. The door was closed. Good.

'Hi,' she said, smiling at the bored-looking police officer. It was the same man as last time, so there was a chance he might recognise her.

He did. His face lit up when he saw her. She had obviously brightened his day. 'Hello, Miss. The DCI is in there at the moment. He brought someone along who might be a friend. Be good if we can give our man a name, eh?'

Serena nodded. 'How long has Detective Armstrong been here?'

The police office looked at his watch. 'About fifteen minutes. He won't stay much longer. He never does.'

'I'd better wait until he comes out. I

don't want to interrupt anything. I'll go and get a coffee.'

She was heading back along the corridor when she heard the door open behind her. She didn't know whether to carry on walking, freeze on the spot, or run for it.

'Miss Conti? What are you doing here?'

With all her options gone, she turned slowly to face Jack Armstrong.

'Going to get a coffee,' she said, producing one of her best smiles. She had dressed to impress the door guard. Skinny jeans and a clingy top in burnt orange, high heels and dangly earrings. 'You finished in there?'

His frown deepened. 'I thought I told you . . .'

'Yes?' She cocked her head. 'What did you tell me, detective?'

Armstrong sighed. 'His name is Liam Glass. He's a student at the university. He shares a flat with someone called Michael Astley — and he's still heavily sedated. Anything else?'

'If Liam is still unconscious can I speak to his friend, please?'

'I could say no, but you wouldn't take any notice, so be my guest. He went down to the coffee shop. I have to speak to the doctor but I'll be down in a little while.'

'I'll look forward to seeing you then, detective.'

She watched him stride away down the corridor. Even from the back, he still looked good.

The coffee shop was almost empty. A couple of nurses in uniform sat at a table in the area reserved for staff, and the only other occupants were a woman in her fifties and a young man wearing glasses. Serena helped herself to a mug of coffee and introduced herself to Michael (please call me Mike) Astley. She waited while he thanked her for saving his friend and told her several times how grateful he was.

'All I did was call an ambulance,' she said, after three or four minutes of adulation.

'You saved his life. He'll thank you himself when he can.' The young man shifted uncomfortably on his chair. 'The thing is, I'm going back home tomorrow morning for the summer break. I won't be back for a couple of months and I want him to know I was here, that I did come and see him. Can you make sure he knows?'

'Of course.' Serena realised that would give her a good excuse to come back to the hospital again. 'I'm sure he'll be better soon. Does he have parents or family? Anyone who needs to be notified?'

'The policeman asked me that, as well. His parents are on a cruise at the moment. It may take them a while to get back to England. Liam was going to stay on at the flat.' Mike Astley looked at her earnestly through his thick lenses. 'I've got to wait for the detective to come back but, before he does, I wanted to give you this.'

He stuck his hand in his pocket and pulled out a small phone. 'Liam left this at the flat and I've been carrying it around. I didn't want to give it to the policeman because I don't know what Liam's got on it. Private emails and things, probably. I won't be here when he gets out of hospital so can you look after it for him.' He handed the phone to Serena. 'I turned it off so it won't keep ringing. I wouldn't know what to say to people if they called him.'

She dropped the phone in her bag. 'When did you discover he'd left it behind?'

'The day he disappeared. I went back to the flat at lunchtime. That's when I saw the phone lying on the table. I didn't see Liam for the rest of the day, and he didn't come home that night, so I never got a chance to give it to him.'

'Don't worry, I'll look after it. I'll give it to him as soon as he wakes up.' She couldn't see any reason to mention the phone to the detective. There were a few things on her phone she would rather keep private. 'When did your friend actually go missing?'

Michael shook his head. 'I'm not sure. The policeman came round and found blood on the floor, and I'm sure it wasn't there in the morning, so if it's Liam's blood, he must have gone back to the flat some time that day.'

'You mean your friend was actually attacked in your flat?' That was news to her. She was about to ask another question when Jack Armstrong appeared in the doorway. 'Don't tell him I was asking questions,' she whispered. 'He doesn't like me doing that.'

'I see you two found each other. Good.' The detective looked at Michael. 'You're flatmate is being kept heavily sedated for another two days. I know you'll be gone by then, but the hospital staff have been told to keep you informed. Give them a ring at the end of the week.'

Michael Astley got to his feet. 'Thank you. Is he going to be all right, do you think?'

'The doctor won't commit himself, but no permanent brain damage as far as they can see. Have a good break with your parents, Mr Astley. Can you leave me a phone number in case I think of anything else I need to ask you?'

The young man found a scrap of paper and wrote down his number, handing it to Jack. He gave Serena a grateful nod before he hurried out.'

'Anything I should know about?'

The detective didn't miss a trick. 'Michael couldn't stop thanking me for saving his friend's life.' She sighed dramatically. 'Such is the price of fame.'

He looked her up and down, his eyes lingering on her cleavage. 'Is the dressing up for my benefit?'

She grinned at him. 'No, actually it was for that poor, bored man sitting by the door. I thought I'd brighten up his day.'

'You hoped he'd be so blinded by your . . . beauty, he'd let you into the room.'

'Something like that, yes.'

He raised his eyes lazily to hers, and she noticed again how blue they were. 'Shame to waste it all.'

'Sorry?'

He looked at his watch. 'It's lunch time and I don't want to eat in a hospital. Fancy a bite at the pub over the road?'

Why did he always surprise her? Just when she thought she'd got him figured out, he asked her out to lunch.

'Why not? As long as you pick up the tab.'

It was his turn to grin. 'Deal. As long as you don't eat too much.'

The pub served cold lager and rare-beef sandwiches in thick brown bread. Serena gulped a mouthful of beer and closed her eyes in ecstasy. 'This is great. Thanks.'

Jack added English mustard to his sandwich and Serena wondered how he could taste the beef. She had never acquired a taste for the bright yellow condiment.

He propped his elbows on the table and leant towards her. 'What did he tell you, then?'

'Who?' She tried to sound innocent,

but she knew exactly who he was talking about. She cursed herself for being naive enough to think she was being asked out on a lunch date. All the man wanted was information. As far as he was concerned, well worth the price of a sandwich.

'Michael Astley. You were talking to him for long enough. Did he tell you anything I don't know?'

'I have no idea what you don't know, so I can't answer that question. Besides, it was a private conversation.'

He caught her wrist before she could move. 'There is no such thing as a private conversation while I am investigating this case. A man nearly died — may still die — and you're still at risk.' He let go of her and leant back in his chair. 'This is not the time to play games with me.'

She rubbed her wrist where his fingers had left a red mark. 'You're the one playing games, Jack. You let me talk to Mike because you knew he might let something slip. Well he didn't. And if he had, regardless of men burglarising the apartment, I still would not tell you. Isn't having me watched enough for you?'

'Watched?'

He looked genuinely perplexed, and her heart skipped a beat. 'The man you have watching the apartment.'

'See!' He clenched his fists but didn't touch her. Instead moved closer until his nose was almost touching hers. 'This is what happens when you keep your little secrets. I tried to requisition an officer to keep an eye on you, but the Chief wasn't having any of it. You're not important enough. So who do you think is watching your apartment?'

'I don't know.' She swallowed. Those pale eyes had ice in them. 'It's probably nothing. Someone meeting a girl, or gone outside for a quick smoke. He stubbed out his cigarette. Made sparks. That's how I noticed him.'

'But you didn't say anything to me.'

'No.' She dropped her eyes before she turned into a popsickle. 'I thought he was a policeman. I thought you knew he was there.'

Jack sighed. 'Well, I didn't. I'll check to see if any of the neighbours have seen a man loitering outside the apartments. 'I'll need you to show me exactly where he was standing, so I'd better follow you home.'

'I've got to work this afternoon. I have a client to see. I've already cancelled once and I'm only in England for a limited period.'

'What time did you see this prowler?'

'When I was going to bed, I think. I don't know. It wasn't that late. Eleven, maybe. But he could have been there some time.'

'I'll come round later, then. That way, I might catch him in the act.' He took her hand again, this time more gently. 'And don't keep secrets, Serena. It could kill you.'

7

Serena got home from work late. Hot and hungry. The CEO of Dream Homes had insisted they sit outside in the courtyard of his office building so he could smoke. Her business suit felt like a duvet after half an hour in the full sun and her hair and clothes had soaked up the smell of tobacco like a sponge. Besides that, it was difficult to see the pictures on her laptop, which rather defeated the object of a full-colour presentation. But she had sold a trial run of the graphics package, which was what really counted. Her boss would be pleased with her.

Simon wasn't home, so she stepped out of her clothes in the bathroom and stood under the shower, turning the water on full. The weather was certainly fickle. Cold one minute and hot the next. Ten minutes later she felt much better — until she checked the messages on the landline and wished she hadn't. Never mind, that little problem could wait for later.

The doorbell rang just as she was slipping on a fresh pair of jeans. She pulled on a tank top and wrapped her dripping hair in a towel. Simon didn't usually forget his key. Then she remembered Jack Armstrong saying he would come round later. Not this early, surely?

She caught a glimpse of herself in the mirror as she hurried towards the front door. No makeup, wet hair and bare feet. Great!

He didn't say anything when she opened the door, but he smiled, and she immediately wanted to hit him.

'I thought you meant later. I wasn't expecting you.

'Pity. I thought you'd scrubbed up especially for me. I did mean later. I've got Nina in the car with me at the moment. I want you to show me exactly where you saw this stalker. I presume he doesn't hang around in the daytime. We didn't spot anyone lurking.'

'I don't know what he does. I only caught a glimpse of him. Just a shape in the dark.' She hadn't thought of the man as a stalker — until now.

'But two nights running. Hiding in the bushes.'

'Maybe he stubs a cigarette out at the same time every night.' She waved her hands. 'I don't know. Perhaps he smokes pot, and that's why he stays out of sight.' Her wet hair was dripping down the back of her neck. 'This is why I didn't say anything, because whatever I say you bump it up out of all proportion.'

'I expect Liam Glass was thinking the same thing when he got beaten up. Put some shoes on your feet and show me where this pot-smoker was standing.' When she didn't move, he added, 'Please?'

Grumbling, she gave her hair another rub and pushed her feet into her slippers. At least she was dressed.

Going outside wrapped in a towel would have upset Simon even more. She shuffled through the gravel with Jack right behind her. She could see Nina watching from the parked car and could imagine the smirk on the woman's face.

'Of course,' Jack said mildly, as she pointed out the shady corner, 'I suppose it could have been a reporter waiting for a shot of the local hero.'

She scowled at him. 'I'm sure it was nothing. Just someone having a quiet cigarette.'

'We'll see.' He gave her a mock salute and got back in the unmarked police car with Nina. 'I'll be back.'

She was sure he was still grinning as he drove away, but she didn't hang around to find out. She needed time to put on makeup and dry her hair before he came back again.

Simon arrived half an hour later bearing pizzas, so dinner was easy, but explaining the detective's visit wasn't quite so easy.

'So we've got a stalker, and you didn't think there was any need to tell me. What were you trying to do, Serena? Spare my feelings? I live here too, remember. The apartment actually belongs to me, but for some reason you didn't bother to tell me my life may be in danger.' He threw knives and forks onto the table with a clatter. 'Is this is ever going to end? Or is it just going to get worse each day?'

Serena put the pizza on a plate. 'This isn't my fault.'

'Well it certainly isn't mine!'

He cut the pizza with such gusto, Serena winced. Should she tell him the next bit of news while he was already cross, or wait until he'd calmed down and then upset him again? Might as well get it all over at once.

'Mother's booked her flight. She'll be here next week.' One look at his face told her she should have waited. 'I'm sorry, but it's a done thing now. She's bought her ticket and she's flying over here whatever we do, so you might as well enjoy your food.'

He put down the pizza cutter and ran a hand through his hair. 'I can't cope with both of you. Not at the same time.'

'I'll move out. I can stay in a hotel for a couple of weeks and then I'll take her back with me.'

'No,' Simon said hastily. 'Quite honestly, Serena, I'd rather have you staying here than her.'

As backhanded compliments go, she thought, that was a good one. 'You haven't seen her for a couple of years.'

'Exactly. And I still remember what it was like.' He sighed. 'But there are two beds in your room. I suppose we could manage for a few days.'

'No way! I don't like sharing a *house* with my mother. I refuse to share a bedroom.'

'Doesn't she have friends here in England, then? Someone we can palm her off on?' He gulped his wine like lemonade. 'She's your responsibility, Serena. She's only coming to England because you got your name in the paper.'

'I'll sort something out,' Serena told him without much conviction.

Simon was right, she was responsible for the upheaval in his life so she had to do what she could, but there was no way she was sharing a bedroom with her mother.

She looked at her watch. Jack should be here any minute. Would he have Nina with him, she wondered, or would he be by himself? He had said he preferred to work alone, and she wasn't really surprised. He wouldn't get many volunteers.

He didn't arrive until 10.30 and she was beginning to think he wasn't going to turn up. Simon had already started yawning. Jack came alone, and walked into the apartment without an invitation. Dressed all in black, he looked like something from a James Bond movie — and just as menacing. She had worried he didn't carry a gun, but perhaps he didn't need one. One glance from those icy blue eyes might be enough.

'Hi. Sorry to spoil your evening, Mr Prescott. I won't take up too much of your time.' He turned to Serena. 'I knocked a few doors with Nina earlier on. No one has seen anyone hanging around. No new faces in the area. It's pretty quiet round here, a nice neighbourhood and not much trouble to speak of. But the house right next door is empty and the police have been called out because of noise. The local kids using it as a clubhouse. The kids have gone, but there's still easy access, like no glass in the windows.' He paused. 'And lots of cigarette butts lying around.'

'Probably a vagrant,' Serena suggested hopefully. 'Someone wanting somewhere dry and warm.'

'The cigarettes are one of the more expensive brands.'

'Someone gave them to him,' she said, a little desperately now. 'Or he stole them. That's more likely, isn't it?'

'About as likely as the hobo suggestion.' He gave Serena a grin that had her looking for his dorsal fin. 'I'll be off on my scavenger hunt, then. If you see anyone lurking about outside, it'll be me.'

Serena shut the door behind him and a few minutes later walked into her bedroom. She looked out of the window. There was nothing moving outside as far as she could see, but that was the whole point of the operation. Jack didn't want to be seen. She had no idea why she felt so nervous. He was used to this sort of thing. Like Simon said, it was his job, and he looked quite capable of handling most situations. She looked worriedly at the window again. He was out there on his own. Surely he should have back-up?

With a sigh, she walked back into the living room where Simon was nervously tapping his fingers on the arm of the sofa. 'I'll make us a cup of tea.' She was getting used to the British way of coping with stress.

Her phone made her jump. She pulled it from the pocket of her jeans and looked at the screen before holding it to her ear. 'Hello? No Jack isn't here, he's gone outside to look for the . . . OK, if it's that urgent, I'd better go and tell him.'

She turned to Simon. 'That was Nina from the police station. An emergency of some sort. She wants Jack to phone her back pronto.'

'Well, he can't, can he? Because he's out there looking for your stalker.'

'I'll go get him. He won't be far away.'

'You can't, Serena!' Simon sounded appalled. 'It might be dangerous.'

'Of course it's not dangerous,' she answered snappily. 'I'm just going down to the parking area. It's well lit, and Jack's there somewhere.'

She was beginning to think it had all been a big mistake. Some poor man getting away from his wife for a quick smoke. A lot of fuss about nothing.

She pulled on a jacket and took the lift down to the entrance lobby. Stepping outside, she realised what a lot of unlit corners there were. The parking lot was butted up against the garden of the house next door where she had seen the smoking man, and that corner was particularly dark. Large overhanging trees obscured the lights and shadows danced on the tarmac when the branches moved. A breeze ruffled the leaves and they hissed reprovingly.

Wishing she had listened to her brother, she walked slowly towards the dark corner. This is what people did in movies. People she always called stupid.

The space under the trees was empty. Standing still, she tipped her head to one side. There had been a sound from the garden of the house next door. A large hedge acted as a boundary, but there was a gap big enough for someone to slip through. She peered into the darkness. That sound again. Someone moving. Probably Jack.

Now came decision time. Push through the gap in the hedge or go back to the apartment. She risked a whisper. 'Jack?'

Nothing.

Nina had sounded anxious on the phone. An emergency, she said. Something that needed Jack's attention right now. Not something that could wait until he'd finished creeping about in the grounds of an empty house looking for a man who wasn't there.

Serena wished she'd asked exactly what the emergency was. Had Liam Glass been attacked again? Or was it something completely different. A man with a gun holding someone hostage, or a traffic accident with bodies all over the road. She closed her eyes and forced the visions out of her head. All she had to do was go through the gap in the hedge and find him. He couldn't be far away.

Easier said than done. The hedge had spikes. For a moment she thought it was razor wire, but no, it was just a very hostile bush. Something clawed at her hair and she almost screamed, stopping herself at the last minute. Don't be an idiot, she told herself. It was a branch.

Just a branch. Another shove and she was through. She could see the house looming in front of her — and a light flickering through one of the gaps where a window should have been. Jack must be in there. He would have seen off any intruders by now.

She walked forwards with more confidence. Just find him and go back. That was all she had to do.

The light went out as she got nearer to the house, but she had already seen a shape moving inside one of the downstairs rooms. The front door was hanging off its hinges, providing easy access. Better than trying to climb through a window. Things crunched under her feet, and she was glad she was wearing trainers rather than slippers. Bits of wallpaper hung from the walls like wilted flower petals, and a piece of flex dangling from the ceiling still held a light bulb. The place smelt of decay and other things she didn't want to give a name to.

She had been standing still for a

couple of minutes, waiting for her eyes to become accustomed to the dark, before she heard the noise again. The creak of a floorboard upstairs.

The obvious thing to do was call out. But what if it wasn't Jack? What if it was the smoking man? Or, even worse, some drunken squatter? A little voice in her head told her now was the time to turn around and go back, but she had come this far . . . She decided she would shout as loudly as she could and be ready to run like hell. If it was Jack in the room upstairs, fine. If not, she still had plenty of time to get away.

She crept to the bottom of the stairs. Someone was still moving around up there, but trying not to make a noise. It had to be Jack.

She had just taken a breath to shout his name when a hand clamped over her mouth and nose. Her gasp of shock turned into a gasp for air. Panicking, she drove her elbow backwards into something soft and was rewarded with a grunt of pain. She was about to do the same again when her captor whispered in her ear.

★ ★ ★

'Pack it in, Serena,' Jack Armstrong rubbed his stomach with his free hand. 'It's me. Jack.' He felt her go slack and removed his hand from her mouth. At least she hadn't bitten him. 'Don't make a sound. There's someone upstairs.'

She nodded, her eyes wide. He held up his hand to tell her to stay where she was and then he started up the stairs. He doubted the intruder had a gun and he knew he was more than a match for most villains. Besides, he had caught a glimpse of the man earlier and knew he was dealing with someone of only average build. As soon as he entered the house, the man had disappeared upstairs.

He had barely reached the halfway point on the staircase when a dark shape going at full speed barrelled past him, knocking him off his feet. He fell backwards, but managed to roll down the last few stairs and was on his feet within seconds. He ignored Serena's squeak of fright and raced to the front door. When he heard a motorbike engine growl to life, he knew he was too late.

He closed his eyes for a moment. He knew the aftermath of an incident like that would leave him high on adrenalin and he needed a moment to calm down. Otherwise he was going to take his anger out on Serena Conti.

She moved towards him tentatively. 'Are you OK? You took quite a tumble.'

'I'm just fine.' He brushed the dust and muck off his black sweatshirt and jeans. 'What exactly are you doing here? If I hadn't been around you might have got yourself killed.'

'I know. And if I hadn't been around, you might have caught the guy. 'I'm sorry, Jack. I got a call from Nina. She wants you to call her back. She said it was an emergency.'

'So you came out here to find me? That was pretty damn stupid.'

He could cheerfully have murdered the silly girl. He had been about to creep upstairs and grab the man, but now the stalker knew someone was on to him he wasn't likely to come back anytime soon.

Jack took Serena by the arm to help her through the doorway and realised she was trembling. He cursed himself for a fool. He should have known how scary it must have been for her, and he probably hadn't helped by grabbing her when she wasn't expecting it.

'Did I hurt you? I had to stop you going upstairs.'

She waved her arms at him. 'No, you idiot, you didn't hurt me. You just scared me half to death. I thought it was you upstairs, so I didn't know who'd grabbed me. I thought it was the stalker.'

'Whoever the stalker was, I've lost him,' he told her bitterly. 'Sometimes I wonder if you *have* a brain in that pretty little head of yours. I'm not going to get another chance at him now, am I?'

'So it's my fault you weren't quick enough to catch him?'

'Basically, yes.'

He saw her eyes flash in the dark and remembered the elbow in his stomach, but he still didn't move quickly enough to stop her slapping his face. He had a sudden urge to put her over his knee and slap her bottom until she begged for mercy, but he also had the sense to realise she was as hyped up as he was.

She was standing facing him, her feet apart, her hands clenched into fists at her sides, and he thought for a moment she was going to have another go at him, but she suddenly crumpled.

As soon as he saw the tears, common sense went out of the window. He caught hold of her and pulled her into his arms, letting her sob against his chest. A few seconds later she quietened and started to pull away, but he held on to her, not quite ready to let her go.

When she raised her head to look at him, he gave in to impulse and kissed her.

Big mistake.

He hadn't expected her to kiss him back. In fact, he had been expecting another slap. But her mouth was as eager as his and he had to fight to keep himself under control. He wanted to blame it on adrenalin, on the moment of danger, on anything else he could think of. But there was no word for the blast of heat that took the breath from his body and left him senseless.

With a supreme effort of will, he untangled himself from her and held her at arms length. She blinked at him as if she had just woken from a deep sleep, and shook her head.

'What just happened?'

'I have no idea. But this is probably not the best place to find out.'

He looked round the dark and dismal room and the smells started to invade his nostrils again. A few moments ago he would have sworn he could smell lilac. She was a witch, and if he wanted to do his job he needed to get her out of his system. How he was going to do that, he would work out later, when he had a clearer head.

They walked back to the apartment in silence and Simon let them in.

'I was about to come out and look for you. Then I thought it would be silly for us all to be creeping about in the dark. What happened, Serena? You said you were just going to deliver a message.'

'I did. I delivered the message.'

When Jack realised she wasn't going to say any more, he stepped in. 'Serena was right about someone being in the empty house. I almost caught him, but he got away on a motorbike.'

'Not a squatter, then?'

'No, not a squatter, but not necessarily a stalker, either. I need to go back in daylight and search that house properly. I'll have another quick look around tonight before I go home, because I want to know what he was doing there. When I went in earlier with Nina the rooms were all empty.' He looked worriedly at Serena. 'Your sister's had a bit of a shock,' he told Simon. 'Take care of her.'

As he opened the door to leave, she touched his arm.

'You take care as well, Jack.'

He stood still for a minute before he headed for his car, checking the immediate area. He felt sluggish, not in complete control of his faculties, and he wasn't sure who was to blame. Once in his car he pulled out his phone and called Nina.

'Catch anyone?' Her voice sounded a little sharp.

'Almost, but he got away.'

'A wild goose chase then?'

'Not completely. Your call didn't help. The Conti woman came looking for me and frightened off the intruder. We need to check out that empty house again in daylight. What was so urgent?'

'Liam Glass is awake and talking. I thought you might want to know.'

8

Simon started to lecture her on her stupidity, but then he saw the tear stains on her face and opened his new bottle of brandy instead.

'It was a bit silly, though, you must admit, Serena, going out there in the dark.'

'It was all perfectly fine until that moron grabbed me. He never thinks before he does things.' She touched her lips. 'Everything's on impulse. I can't imagine how he ever became a policeman.' She took a gulp of her brandy and coughed. 'A detective, even! How'd he get to be a detective?'

'He's probably very good at his job. He said you frightened the man away.'

'He would, wouldn't he? The guy actually ran past him on the stairs. A narrow little space like a stairwell and Jack Armstrong still couldn't stop him.

I would have tripped the man up. As it was, by the time our brilliant detective had managed to pick himself up from the bottom of the stairs, the guy had roared away on a motorbike.' She picked up the brandy bottle and topped up her glass. 'A proper detective would have found the motorbike first and disabled it.'

'If he had found it, how would he have known it belonged to the intruder?'

'You're just making excuses for him. Men always stick together. I'm going to bed.'

She walked, with as much dignity as she could muster, into her bedroom and closed the door. She found she was crying again for some reason and threw herself on the bed. This was ridiculous. What on earth was wrong with her? OK, so she had suffered a bit of a shock, and the dark house had been scary — but the damned man had kissed her senseless and then hardly spoken to her. When something like that happens there is supposed to be some follow up. Some sort of communication between the two people involved.

It wasn't as if she'd never been kissed before. Of course she had, hundreds of times. But nothing like that. She'd read about it, but never quite believed it. A Harry met Sally kiss that really did blow your mind.

That made her smile. In reality, it might never happen again, but at least she knew it was out there, waiting.

She dreamt of a dark castle and a man on a horse. There was a serpent as well, but she couldn't see its face because it was wearing a deer-stalker hat.

Chrissie Prescott arrived at 7.30 am in the morning without calling to warn them. She came by taxi with a collection of designer suitcases that had Serena wondering how long she intended to stay.

'Simon darling, I don't have loose change for the cab and I refused to give him my Amex card.' She kissed Serena and plonked herself down on the sofa. 'I need coffee right now or I may just fall apart. The flight was *appalling*.'

'I'm not sure why you're here, Chrissie. Is it a holiday, or what?' She watched Simon head out the door to pay the cab fair and turned back to her mother with a sigh. 'We've both got to work today.'

'You can't possibly go to work as if nothing has happened. The paper said you might be the next victim of this maniac.'

Serena blinked. 'What maniac?'

'Oh, don't play dumb with me, Serena. You know exactly who I mean. The madman who beat up that poor boy.' She looked around. 'Have you got someone guarding you?'

'We're being well looked after, Mother. Someone will no doubt follow me to work. And don't worry about being here alone. A police car will drive by every now and again.'

All more or less true, Serena told herself. Police cars often drove by, and someone in a car was bound to follow her to work. Not necessarily a patrol car, but someone. She tried not to lie to her mother, but Chrissie Prescott was so neurotic Serena had to bend the truth occasionally.

The strange thing was, the next day she *was* followed to work, or she was pretty certain she was. When she parked in the Dream Homes car park, the black SUV that had been behind her all the way from the apartment stopped on the other side of the road. She couldn't see how many people were in the car, and she didn't want to stare, but she had a creepy feeling someone was watching her. It came with the thought that breaking into a run might be a good idea. Besides, the SUV looked remarkably like the one that had turned up the night she found Liam in the ditch. The one with the fake cops inside.

Still spooked, she decided to give Jack Armstrong a call. The least he could do was come and check the car out. Still watching the suspect car, she pulled her phone out of her bag, but as she was about to dial she realised it wasn't her own phone she was holding. It was the one Liam's flat mate had given her. She looked at it in surprise. She had forgotten she still had it.

At that moment one of the men got out of the car, and now there was no doubt in her mind. It was the man she had seen at the hospital when Liam Glass had nearly died. She dropped the phone back in her bag and almost ran into the office block. Once inside, she felt reasonably safe, but she still watched the doors as she hurried towards the lift.

She found Graham Blackwell in his office and tried to forget the car outside. She had agreed to spend several hours with Graham going over the CCG for his computer programme, and she hoped by the time she left the office the big black car would be gone.

She was late leaving and the car park was almost empty. As she walked towards her car she was still thinking about the contract that was so nearly hers. She'd tied up the London office, now all she had to do was get Graham to sign on the bottom line and she could go home, back to Sacramento, and take her mother with her. She had suggested Chrissie book a room at the Premier Inn, but Chrissie wasn't impressed. She was probably in the process of booking herself into an exorbitantly expensive hotel right this minute.

Lost in her thoughts, Serena was quite unprepared for the sight of someone leaning on her car. A moment of panic quickly turned into annoyance when she saw who it was.

'What are you doing here?'

'Leaning on your car.'

'Why are you leaning on my car?'

'Don't look now, but a man in a four-by-four is watching you from the other side of the road.'

She looked across the road. It was the same black SUV, and she could see at least one man inside.

She couldn't believe Jack was just standing there. She looked at him incredulously. 'He followed me this morning. He must have been here all the time I've been inside, and I expect the other guy's around somewhere. Why don't you pick them up?'

'Tell me what they've done that's against the law, and I will.'

'They're stalking me! You know that. They tried to kill Liam Glass and burglarised Simon's place. What more do you need?'

He looked at her sadly and shook his head. 'It would be nice to have a little tinsy bit of evidence to back that up. Think about it, Serena. *You* say you saw them at the scene of the incident. *You* say you saw one of them at the hospital. You are *assuming* the same men broke into your brother's apartment. What do you want me to do, knock on the car window and ask them to sign an assumption?'

She waved her hands at him. 'There

must be something you can do.'

'I already did it. I phoned in their registration number. It's being checked right now.'

'They'll change cars.'

'Possibly, but we'll still know who that one belongs to.' He held open her car door. 'I'm very serious about this, Serena. If there's anything you know you haven't told me, anything that relates to those two men, you're not doing yourself any favours by keeping it to yourself.'

She shook her head as she slid into her car. 'I don't know anything else.' She pulled her skirt down over her knees. 'And you didn't answer my question. Why are you following me?'

He grinned at her, his eyes lingering on her legs. 'I wasn't following you. I was following *them* following you.' He moved back and slammed her door, but as she was about to drive away he motioned for her to wind down her window.

'If you fancy a trip to the hospital

tomorrow morning, Liam Glass is awake. He's not fully recovered and he's not making a lot of sense, but a visit from you might help.'

'Help who? Or should that be whom? Sorry, but as you pointed out, my English grammar is not so hot.'

She was pleased the student was conscious, but if she decided to visit Liam it wasn't going to be because Jack told her to. She was nearly home before the full impact of what had happened hit her. She was being followed by two potential murderers and she wondered what would have happened if Jack Armstrong hadn't shown up when he did.

She glanced anxiously over her shoulder, remembering a film where a man had hidden in the back of the car and suddenly appeared behind the driver. She was annoyed she had allowed the men to spook her, but now her mother was in England as well, and she couldn't bear to think of her mother being harmed because of something she had done. Why on earth had she stopped on that road? She could so easily have driven on. But goodness knows what would have happened to Liam Glass if she had. He might be dead by now. And — the little thought crept unbidden into her head — she might never have met Jack Armstrong.

As she parked her car outside the apartment, she noticed one of the lights had blown again. She got out slowly, not relishing the walk across the car park in the dark. Reaching into the back of the car, she grabbed her purse with one hand and her laptop case with the other and got ready to run. She hated this feeling of vulnerability. She had always been determined not to become a victim like her mother.

She heard running footsteps and turned with a gasp, but the man who snatched her bag was so quick it was all over in seconds. At first she thought he was after her laptop and clutched the case fiercely to her side, but he grabbed her handbag, pulling it off her arm before she could get a proper grip. When he took a swipe at her, she decided a cheap purse wasn't worth a broken jaw and let him take it. Everything in it could be replaced.

She was locking her car door with a trembling hand when she heard a commotion outside the entrance. A few moments later Jack Armstrong appeared carrying her purse.

'This yours?'

She gave him a shaky smile as she took it. 'Thanks. Did you catch him?'

'Yeah. He's locked in my car at the moment. But he's not one of the men who followed you to work.'

'Then who the hell is he? Exactly how many people *are* following me?'

'Exactly?' He considered her question thoughtfully. 'I can't give you an exact number, but I would say, given the evidence, definitely as many as three.'

She sighed. 'I'm not in the mood, Jack. Just a pick-pocket, then?'

'A paid pick-pocket. Someone gave him fifty quid to grab your handbag. Said they'd be waiting — and watching.'

'So? Who paid him?'

'He doesn't know, so neither do I. I can make a calculated guess, but still no evidence.'

She leant against the door of her car. For some reason her eyes wouldn't focus properly. 'I think I need to sit down.'

He caught her as her legs buckled and picked her up in his arms. Carrying her to a patch of grass by the door to the apartments, he sat her down, supporting her with one arm and pushing her head down between her knees with the other.

Finding that position quite painful Serena tried to sit up but he wouldn't let go of her.

'Keep your head down.'

'It hurts,' she mumbled. Her face was being pressed so hard against her tight skirt she wondered if he was trying to suffocate her. 'I'm OK now. Really I am. And I can't breathe.'

He let go reluctantly. 'Let me help you indoors.'

She shook her head violently. 'No! My mother will have a fit if she thinks I've been mugged. She's freaked out enough as it is. I just need a minute.'

He still had one arm round her and he didn't seem in any hurry to let go. 'What have you got in that bag?'

'Nothing out of the ordinary. The usual rubbish. Cosmetics, wallet, phone.' She handed him her bag. 'You're welcome to look.'

She didn't think he would, but he actually rummaged around inside. After a minute he handed it back.

'I don't think he had time to take anything, but you'd better check.'

'I will when I get inside.' She started to struggle to her feet. 'I don't know why you're here, Jack. I'm grateful you were following me again, but I don't need a bodyguard.'

He kept his arm round her as he

helped her up. 'You have to take care of yourself, Serena. I can't watch you every minute of the day. I want to catch those two villains but I can't lock them up without evidence, so in the meantime I need you to be careful.'

'I don't know why you care so much about me.' Standing on tiptoe she kissed him lightly on the lips. 'But thanks, anyway.'

'That's not good enough. Not for someone who cares about you.' He had both arms round her now, holding her against him. 'I'm sure you can do better than that.'

She blamed her wobbly legs. If she tried to push him away she might fall over. Besides, it felt so good in his arms.

He kissed her lightly at first, his lips barely brushing hers, but she wanted more. She slid her hands up his chest and gently brushed the back of his neck with the tips of her fingers. His immediate response had her smiling against his mouth. She felt empowered, in control for once, and that was incredibly sexy. But a few minutes later everything changed. He backed her up against the wall and plundered her mouth until her brain turned to mush. What had she been thinking? Jack Armstrong would never let her take control — and right this minute she didn't care.

Somewhere deep inside her a tiny spark of commonsense must have been hiding and, much to her disappointment, it chose that minute to surface. She felt him start to unbutton her blouse and slid her hands down to his belt buckle, but a little voice inside her screamed 'Have you lost your mind? This is a car park!' She moved her hands back to his shoulders and reluctantly pushed him away.

'Not here, Jack. My brother lives here — and you're a policeman.'

He looked at her, his eyes glazed. It took him a moment to focus, and then he laughed quietly. 'Behaviour unbecoming to an officer of the law. If you hadn't stopped me it might have been indecent exposure as well. Sorry.'

'Don't say sorry. If I remember rightly, I started it.' She managed to ease herself away from the wall, not at all sure if her legs would hold her. 'I could have stopped you sooner.'

'If you'd wanted to.'

'If I'd wanted to.' She took a breath. 'But there's so much going on in my life at the moment I don't think I can cope with a romantic relationship.'

'Is that what it is?' He tipped his head on one side to study her. 'I was trying to steer away from the obvious. I didn't think you'd find a car park particularly romantic.'

'Or a hospital room. I must admit your choice of settings for seduction are pretty unique.' She gave him a rueful smile. 'I need to get inside, Jack. Let's sort this mess out first and then see if we can remember where we were just now.'

He walked with her to the doorway. 'I know exactly where I was. Just two buttons away from heaven.'

★　★　★

When Serena opened the door to the apartment, she could smell food. Chrissie Prescott had dinner on the stove, a casserole of some sort, and it smelt really good. Her brother was laying the table. He usually ate before he came home, or ordered something on his mobile phone, and she had been living on Pizza and Indian take-away. Now there was real food in the house.

They washed everything down with red wine and shared a tub of ice cream, and Chrissie positively glowed with pleasure. She was always happiest when she was busy, and Serena was glad she hadn't mentioned the bag snatcher.

Simon made his excuses and went off to meet his girlfriend, and Serena could almost hear his sigh of relief as he disappeared out of the door. She sat on the sofa opposite her mother, determined to have a pleasant evening, come what may. For some reason an evening at home with her mother usually ended in a row.

It hadn't always been like that. Chrissie, with her blond hair and voluptuous body, had been a happy person until her executive position had been terminated. Now they were relying on Serena's salary to pay the bills, and Chrissie had been forced to give up most of her expensive leisure activities.

'Rory was asking after you, Serena,' Chrissie said.

As far as Serena was concerned, Rory was a klutz with more money than brain. She wasn't interested. When he asked her to marry him she had laughed at him, but he had accused her of playing hard to get.

'You know what I think of Rory.'

'A lot of girls would jump at the chance to marry Rory Summers.' Chrissie held up her hand. 'You should at least give him a chance, Serena.'

'Why?'

'Because he's rich and we could do with the extra money. I know that sounds mercenary, but we have to be realistic. His father owns a real-estate company, and Rory is going to take over the business in a few years.'

Serena looked at her mother and tried very hard not to lose her temper. 'Why don't *you* marry someone rich, Mother? You may not have any money but you still have your body. Find out what that's worth, why don't you?'

She took one look at her mother's face and wished she could take the words back. With a sinking feeling she realised it was all happening again, and this time it was her fault. She remembered Simon had a new bottle of brandy and she found it in a kitchen cabinet. She poured them both a generous portion and carried the glasses back into the room where her mother was dabbing her eyes with a tissue.

'I'm sorry. I didn't want to start an argument and what I said was uncalled for. I'm really sorry.' She handed her mother the glass of brandy and turned on the television. 'Let's sit and watch the TV until it's time to go to bed. There's no need for you to find a hotel, there's plenty of room in with me.'

While Serena was searching for a programme or a film that would suit them both, the local news came on. According to the report, the police were hunting two men in connection with the critical condition of a local student. The camera showed a shot of the hospital entrance and then switched to the parkland surrounding the university.

Serena heard her mother catch her breath and thought it was another sob, but when she turned round Chrissie was staring at the television screen as if she had just seen a ghost.

'What is it?' Serena asked, alarmed. The colour had drained from her mother's face and she looked as if she was about to faint. 'What's the matter? Do you feel ill?'

Chrissie reached for her brandy glass. She hesitated a moment and then downed the golden liquid in one gulp.

'No, it's nothing, honey. I thought I saw someone I knew. I'm sure I was mistaken, but I still feel a bit shaken up.' She waved the empty glass in the air. 'Can I have another drink, please.'

Serena poured another half-inch of brandy into her mother's glass. 'It must have been a shock. You look really pale. Who do you think you saw?'

Chrissie got shakily to her feet, holding on to the back of the sofa for support. 'I was mistaken. I think I'll go to bed, Serena. I really don't feel up to watching TV. I'm sorry, dear.'

Serena gave her mother a hug, something she hadn't done for a while. 'Please tell me who you saw, Mom, otherwise I shall worry all night. Is it someone we should be afraid of?'

Chrissie closed her eyes. 'No, he wouldn't harm you, but it couldn't have been him. It's impossible. He doesn't know where you live.'

'Who? Who is it you're talking about?' Serena wanted to give her mother a shake. 'Who did you see?'

Chrissie opened the door to the bedroom and then turned back to look at her daughter.

'I thought I saw your father.'

9

Serena had moved her session with Graham Blackwell to the afternoon. She had a meeting with some other executives later in the week, and somehow she had to put a portfolio together before then. Normally she would be excited about the work, but today the whole idea of a digitally created home on a screen seemed particularly trivial.

She was worried about her mother. Chrissie was definitely getting worse.

After hearing about her husband's death and then losing her job, both within the same year, Chrissie had been severely depressed, but counselling and a variety of pills had seemed to be working. Serena had felt optimistic enough about her mother's progress to come to England, never expecting Chrissie to follow her across the ocean.

Now her mother had started seeing things.

The best advice she could give herself was to get the job with Dream Homes done and get her mother back to Sacramento.

She parked in the hospital car park and collected a ticket. Jack Armstrong had asked her here, so he should pay for the parking meter. They let you in for free, and then gave you a heart attack with the amount it cost to get out again. Touting for business, maybe?

Smiling to herself, she hurried to the elevator. A figure in a white coat running across the foyer towards her almost had her leaping out again. But this was a genuine doctor who gave her a sympathetic smile when he saw the look of fear on her face. A panic attack in a hospital is probably not that unusual.

She found Liam's room without any trouble, but there was no policeman on guard and the elderly occupant of the room looked nothing like the student. She looked again at the number on the door, wondering if there had been some sort of emergency. Hoping Liam had just been moved to another room she checked the rooms up and down the corridor, getting suspicious looks from the occupants. Perhaps he had been moved back into intensive care — or died during the night? Anything was possible.

Nurses were all over the place until you needed one. Fearing the worst, she made her way back to the nurses' station at the entrance to the ward and asked what had happened to the injured student.

The young nurse smiled at her. 'Oh, that dishy detective had him moved. Wanted his name taken down from the board as well. He's not on our ward any more. None of us up here know where he is.' She picked up the phone. 'Hang on a minute, I have a number to call if anyone asks for him.'

In case the bogus doctor has another go, Serena thought. She gave her name to the girl, mentioning that Jack

Armstrong had asked her to come to the hospital. Damn the man, the least he could have done was let her know Liam had been moved. She'd been wandering around like an idiot.

The student had a room all to himself in the private sector. There was no policeman outside the door, but a man in hospital whites sat just inside, writing diligently in an official looking document. He looked up as Serena entered the room, immediately on the alert. He must have been told to treat women with as much suspicion as men.

'Detective Armstrong asked me to come and see Mr Glass,' she said, going all formal because she was nervous.

Liam Glass was propped up in bed, looking a lot better than when she had seen him last. The swelling on his face had gone down and the stitches in his lip had been removed, but his eyes were closed and he looked as if he was asleep. She supposed a brain haemorrhage took it out of you.

'Miss Conti? I was told to expect

you.' The man in the white coat smiled apologetically. 'Do you have some form of identification?'

She always carried her passport with her when she was in England. Now she handed it to the policeman and waited while he went through it page by page, eventually checking her photograph.

'Good photo,' he said, handing the passport back with a smile. 'In mine, I look like a serial killer.'

'Damn it, Steve!' Jack said from the doorway. 'I knew I'd seen you somewhere before.'

'Ha ha.' The man got to his feet. 'Now you're back perhaps I can grab a bite to eat.'

Jack motioned her to the chair by the bed. 'I told Liam you were coming to see him. I was hoping he'd remember you. The doctors don't think his brain is permanently damaged so his memory should come back to him in time. His parents will be here tomorrow, that should help, but we really need to know what happened before you found him.'

'Can he hear you?' It bothered her that they were talking about Liam as if he was still in a coma.

'Probably. But he's in that place between sleeping and waking. He can hear us, but he doesn't really care what we're talking about. Every now and again he opens his eyes and then goes back to sleep again.'

'Do they know what caused his injuries?'

The detective smiled. 'Not you, if that's what you're worrying about. He had a traumatic blow to the head, which might have been caused by a fall, and a while later it seems he jumped, or fell, from a moving car. Obviously not one of his best days.'

'So he wasn't beaten up?'

Jack Armstrong rubbed a hand over his jaw. The dark stubble almost a beard. 'To be honest, we don't know. The doctor won't commit himself, but it looks as if hitting the road at a fairly high speed did most of the damage.'

Serena looked at the sleeping man.

He had a white bandage round his head that stopped just above his eyes. His eyelids kept twitching as if he was dreaming. 'What would make him jump from a moving car?'

'Something that was worse than *not* jumping from a moving car. If we can get any sense out of him, we might find out. That's why I asked you to come here. He seems to like talking to you.'

'He's asleep.'

'Then wake him up.' Jack put a hand in his pocket and pulled out a phone. 'I had it on vibrate.' He glanced at the dial. 'Look, I have to take this outside. Talk to him, Serena. See if you can get any sense out of him.'

The detective disappeared through the door and left Serena alone with the injured student. She felt her heart rate quicken. What if the bogus doctor came back? What was she supposed to do? What if it was a real doctor and she went running up the corridor screaming like a psycho? They'd check her past history and find out her mother was nuts, seeing things on TV that weren't really there. Jack wouldn't be any help. He'd probably already decided she was short of a few brain cells. She'd let him kiss her, hadn't she?

A sound from the bed had her swinging round. Liam Glass had his eyes open. He licked dry lips and nodded towards the water jug on his side table. She half-filled the beaker and helped him get the straw in his mouth. He took a few sips and handed the cup back to her.

'You.'

She nodded. Get him to talk, Jack had said. Not so easy if all Liam could manage was one-word sentences. 'You remember me?'

A slight movement of his head could have been a nod. 'When . . . is . . . it?'

She took the question literally. 'You've been in here for over a week. You hit your head.' She wasn't very good at this. 'Your parents are coming to see you tomorrow.'

He looked puzzled so she tried again.

Where the hell was Jack? 'Your friend, Michael, came to see you. He's away at the moment. Do you remember Michael?'

Liam moved in the bed. He looked agitated and she wondered if the questions were upsetting him, so she decided to try another tack. She took the phone Michael had given her out of her bag and held it up in front of him.

'This is your phone. You left it behind at the flat you share with Michael.'

The screech of the monitor startled her so much she gave a little squeak of fright. A red light was flashing behind Liam, he was twitching and his eyes had rolled up into his head.

She looked round frantically. There was a call-bell somewhere. She remembered seeing it the last time she came, but this room was different, the bed the other way round. Someone came running before she had time to scream for help and pushed a buzzer on the wall — and then everything happened at once.

'Out! Everyone out! We need room in here.'

She recognised the resuscitation trolley from TV movies and tried to get out of the way, but there seemed to be people everywhere. Someone grabbed her arm and pulled her out of the room just as the policeman in the white coat came racing back in. She hoped there was order somewhere in the chaos. She was hanging on to her breakfast by a thread, not sure if she was going to pass out or throw up. Hoping it was the former.

Jack let go of her arm and caught her as she tottered. 'Sit down before you fall down.' He dragged her into a curtained side bay and shoved her into a chair. 'What the hell happened in there?'

'I don't *know* what happened. I was talking to Liam and he started shaking and then the alarm went off . . . ' She snorted back a sob. 'I don't know what happened. He isn't dead, is he?'

Jack walked to a water-cooler in the

corner and filled a plastic cup. 'Sip, don't gulp. If you feel faint again put your head between your knees. You should know the drill by now, you've had plenty of practice.'

She sipped the water and felt her blood start to circulate again. She must look really stupid. A typical hysterical female. She always managed to look stupid in front of Jack Armstrong.

Taking a deep breath, she handed back the cup. 'I'm fine now, thanks.'

'Good. So now you can answer some questions. Something must have triggered that attack. Something you said or something you did. We're going to go over everything that happened after I walked out of the room, and you're going to remember every single thing.'

She felt her lip quiver. It did that when she was about to cry, and she must not, on any account, cry right now. He was watching her, staring at her face, and she knew the tears she had been holding back were about to overflow.

It was all his fault. He should never have left her alone in that room — and he knew it. That was why he was being so horrid. Not because Liam had nearly died — yet again — but because he felt guilty.

'I don't feel like talking right now. I've had a shock and I need to go home.'

He walked over and pulled the curtain across the doorway. 'You're not going anywhere until I know what started that fit. Something triggered it. What upset him, Serena? You must know. You were right next to him.'

'I — don't — know,' she said, very slowly and distinctly in case he didn't get it first time around. 'Just after you left, he opened his eyes and asked for water. I filled a cup and helped him get the straw in his mouth. He only took a few sips. I told him his friend had been in to see him, but he just looked confused, so I told him I had his cell phone . . . '

'What cell phone? Liam Glass's

mobile phone? Damn! I was sure he must have one somewhere. How did you get hold of it?'

He looked as if he was about to shake her and she moved back in the chair. Not because she was scared of him, but because he was shouting at her again, and that really pissed her off. 'Stop shouting! I'm fed up with you shouting at me. His flatmate, Michael whatever-his-name-is, found Liam's phone. He couldn't give it back because he's off home for the vacation, so he gave it to me.'

'And you've been carrying it around all this time and never thought to mention it?' Jack ran a hand through his hair, making it stand on end. 'Why would you do that? Are you deliberately trying to sabotage my investigation?'

'Don't be ridiculous.' She knew her voice was shaking but she didn't seem able to get it under control. 'Liam's phone has nothing to do with your investigation. I was looking after it until I could give it back to him, and I'm getting really fed up . . . ' her voice caught, ' . . . with you shouting at me over nothing.' She fished in her purse for a tissue and then got to her feet and walked across the room to the water cooler. 'I need another drink of water.'

He followed her. 'What did you do with the phone, Serena? Where is it?'

That was the problem. She had no idea. She had discovered it was missing when she felt in her purse for the tissue. Maybe she'd dropped it when Liam had his fit. Goodness, there had been more important things to think about than a phone. Liam Glass had been about to die.

'I don't know.' She turned to face Jack Armstrong. 'I think I might have dropped it.'

'Where? Back in the room? Where did you drop it?'

She waved her hands in the air, feeling the tears start and unable to stop them this time. 'I told you, I don't know. It was all so . . . '

He caught hold of her arms as if he

was about to shake her, but then he must have seen the tears. She heard him sigh as he pulled her against his chest. She didn't protest. Right now, she needed a cuddle.

He let her snivel for a few minutes, and then gently eased her away, holding her at arms length. She saw the wet patch on his nice white shirt and smiled up at him.

'Sorry.'

'No problem.' Once again, he seemed reluctant to let her go. 'Try and remember to bring more tissues with you next time.'

She waited until he dropped his arms and then helped herself to a handful of wipes from a dispenser on the wall. She blotted her eyes and wiped her nose. 'I hardly ever cried when I was small. I knew it upset Mom. But when I'm with you I do it all the time. I wonder why that is?'

'No idea. I don't usually have that effect on my women.' He pulled back the curtain covering the doorway. 'Stay here, Serena. I'll see if I can find that phone.'

'Just a minute.' She stopped him with a hand on his arm before he disappeared through the doorway. 'What do you mean, *your* women?'

This time he grinned at her, his eyes flashing silver. 'Sorry. Slip of the tongue.'

He came back a few minutes later holding the phone. 'You *had* dropped it. It probably got kicked around a bit . . . ' he pushed a button ' . . . but it's still working.'

She reached out and snatched the phone out of his hand. 'What's on there is private. Liam is a victim, not a suspect. You can't confiscate his phone and read his messages without his permission.' Jack tried to take the phone back but she put her hand behind her back. 'I'm serious, Jack. I promised I'd look after it.'

He looked up at the ceiling as if he was asking advice from above. 'But Liam Glass is unconscious again, thanks to you, and Michael Astley has gone on holiday, so how do I ask anyone's permission? That phone may be vital to the case.'

'How can it be?' She took her hand from behind her back but kept the phone out of his reach. The dial had gone dark again.'

'I won't know until I see what's on it, will I?' He moved closer to her. 'Don't worry, I'm not going to try and grab it. Just stand still for a minute and let me look at it. There's something not quite right about that phone. It's too cheap.'

She looked down. 'A throwaway? So what? Lots of people use them.'

'Not over here, they don't. Besides, what student uses a cheap, tacky phone? They need to Google things, check Facebook and Twitter, look up the answers to their exams. This phone could just about make a call. It's a granny phone.'

'So what?' she said again.

'So — I wonder if it really belongs to Liam Glass. Tell me again how you got it.'

At that moment a nurse popped her head through the doorway. 'Sorry, but we need to use this bay. You'll have to go to the waiting room.' She saw the look on Jack Armstrong's face and added a belated 'please'.

He took Serena's arm. 'Liam won't be talking for a while, so how about I buy you a coffee?'

She allowed him to lead her outside to the elevator. 'You owe me, anyway.'

He shook his head and patted the wet patch on his shirt. 'This makes us even.'

Once they were seated in a quiet corner of the restaurant, with two mugs of coffee in front of them, he asked her again about the phone. She had put it between them on the table and now she stared at it. Jack was right, the cheap phone with its small screen was not something a student in the States would ever admit to owning, and it was probably the same here.

Jack was waiting for an explanation and she tried to get her thoughts in order.

'Michael told me he went back to their student accommodation the day Liam went missing, and that's when he found the phone. He guessed it must be Liam's because only the two of them lived in the apartment, and it wasn't his. He was about to leave on vacation and Liam was unconscious, so he gave the phone to me. I promised I'd keep it safe until Liam was better.'

Jack stared at the phone on the table. 'When did Michael go back to the flat? In the evening after classes?'

Serena closed her eyes, trying to remember exactly what Michael had told her. 'No, he said he went back to pick up some papers at lunchtime. That's when he found the phone. He took it back to the university, but Liam wasn't there because he'd gone missing by that time.'

'And now we have reason to believe Liam was attacked at the flat.' He looked across the table at Serena. 'So one of his attackers could have dropped the phone. It's a supermarket cheapy, like your throwaways. Pay-as-you-go. Criminals use them.'

'So that's why you need to look at it and see all his messages?'

'Yes.'

He held out his hand but, again, she moved the phone out of his reach. 'We'll look at it together.'

He sighed, and moved his chair to sit beside her. 'Fair enough, but I'll push the buttons, you can watch.'

He turned the phone on and went into Menu and then Messages. 'There's only one received message on here, and that was the day Liam Glass didn't turn up for classes. That's interesting, isn't it?' He looked at her and sighed. 'I should take this back to the station before I go any further. If it concerns the case, you shouldn't be here.'

She turned in her seat to look back at him, trying not to let those cool blue eyes intimidate her. 'But I've had the phone in my bag all this time and I could've looked at the messages any time. How do you know I didn't?'

'Point taken.' He pushed a button and she heard his intake of breath. She leant closer, her cheek brushing his in her effort to see the tiny screen. There was no message — just six numbers.

361253

Serena couldn't take her eyes from the screen. 'They're the same numbers Liam told me. The phone must belong to him. He must have saved them on there so he wouldn't forget them.'

Jack was playing with buttons. 'No, he didn't save them, someone sent them to him.' He looked up and met Serena's eyes. 'That's if the phone belongs to him.'

'And if it doesn't?'

'Then it might be what those two men have been looking for, and it might be the reason why someone tried to snatch your handbag.'

'So how did Liam get hold of a cell phone belonging to two crooks?'

Jack shook his head. 'We may never know. Unless our victim wakes up and tells us.'

'So what do we do with the phone now?'

'*We* don't do anything with it. *I* take it back to the station and get it looked at. I'll try and find out where it was purchased, but, like I said, it probably came from a supermarket. There'll be no record.'

'All the landline phones over here have an area code and six numbers. It could be a phone number. Can't you trace it?'

'Difficult without an area code.' He stared in to space for a moment. 'What were the words again? The ones Liam Glass said when he was in the ditch?'

'Phone,' she said quietly, 'and left. I thought left was a direction, but Liam could have been saying someone had left a phone. That's how he came to have it, because someone had left it behind somewhere.'

'You should join the police force. You'd make a good detective.'

She leant back in her chair. 'At least it's beginning to make sense.'

'But it's still all speculation; and the phone is worthless on its own, so it must be the numbers that are so important.' He got to his feet. 'Will you be OK now? I need to get back to work.'

She looked at her watch. 'So do I. Keep me in the loop, Jack? I need to know what's going on.'

'No you don't.' He stared at her for a long moment — and then he smiled, and those cool blue eyes warmed to the colour of a summer sky. 'But you never know, I might want to see you again.'

He was gone before she could answer.

10

Back at the police station Nina had irritation written all over her face. 'Where've you been? I've been trying to get you.' She was wearing a red top and the tightest black jeans Jack had ever seen.

He felt a small stab of guilt when he remembered he had turned his phone off in the hospital and not yet turned it on again. But it was only a very small stab.

'So what's the emergency this time?'

'Someone reportedly hanging around the science block on the university campus. Not a student evidently, someone older. I though you'd want to know.'

'Who phoned it in?'

'One of the students. Most of them have left already, but a few stay on for summer school or swatting up for exams.

Because there aren't many students around, a stranger gets noticed.'

Jack dropped into the seat behind his desk. 'Got a phone number for the informant?'

She shook her head. 'The officer who took the call didn't think it was important. He asked for a name, but the student hung up, so he assumed it was a hoax.'

'It may still be nothing, but we might as well go and take a look.'

Nina had perched herself on a corner of his desk. 'Want me to come?'

He looked at her appraisingly. 'If we don't want someone to report us for loitering as well, you'll probably be an asset. You look more like a student than I do.'

She patted his knee as she stood up, her earlier irritation forgotten. 'You can pose as my dad.'

He grabbed his jacket from the back of his chair. 'Don't push your luck.'

Nina was right behind him when he climbed into his car. She had come to him from vice, and sometimes she dressed as if she had never left, but she was a good detective. In a situation like this, when he wasn't sure what he was up against, it was good to have her around.

'Do you think it's the same man who was hanging around the Conti woman's apartment?'

Jack waited while she plugged in her seat belt. 'I've no idea, but I don't believe in coincidences and there may be a third party involved. I'm pretty sure the man in the empty house wasn't one of the two goons who've been following Serena Conti.'

'Because he got the better of you, and a goon couldn't do that, right?'

Jack put his foot down and shot out onto the road. 'Something like that, yes.'

The university parkland basked serenely in the late afternoon sunshine, but the squat, concrete buildings dotted about amongst the trees looked like toys dropped by an untidy giant. A week of heavy rain earlier in the month and then warm sunshine, had given everything a spurt of growth and the grass was already looking unkempt.

'We'll hang about for a bit. The intruder might still be here somewhere.' He pointed to a clump of trees softening the hard lines of a two-story block. 'That's the Science block over there.'

As they started to walk towards the trees, a woman came into view from behind the building. At first sight, Jack would have called her plump, but as she got closer he realised it was more like old-fashioned, Marilyn Monroe voluptuousness. She was probably in her fifties, but if she was a lecturer he might consider taking another degree.

She didn't notice them until the last minute.

'Excuse me,' Jack called out, stopping the woman in her tracks. 'Could we have a quick word?'

For a moment she looked as if she was about to run and Jack wondered why, but she quickly regained her composure and continued walking towards them.

'Of course you may, but I doubt I can help.' She gave Jack a smile that would have melted an iceberg. 'I don't work here. I'm from Sacramento in the United States, and I wanted to see a British university. Besides, the park is so pretty.'

'You're here on a visit?'

She smiled again, and he realised she was completely ignoring Nina. 'Yes. I'm over here visiting my son and daughter.'

Fed up with being left out of the conversation, Nina took her smartphone out of her pocket. 'We're police officers and we're looking for a trespasser. Could I have your name and current address, please?' Her smile wasn't nearly so warm. 'Just so we can eliminate you from our enquiries.'

Jack thought he saw a flicker of fear on the woman's face, but it was gone so quickly he might have imagined it.

'I hope I haven't done anything wrong. I was only looking around. My name is Chrissie Prescott, and my son's address is number five, Chantry House, Maple Street.' She glanced at a gold watch on her wrist. 'I should get back now. My children will be worrying about me.'

'We'll drive you home, Mrs Prescott.' Jack said easily. 'We've held you up, so it's only fair.' He took her arm and felt it tremble. 'Besides, I know your daughter quite well.'

* * *

Serena drove home slowly. Graham Blackwell was about ready to agree to the package she had offered him. All that was left was to convince the other members of the board and then she could think about going home. Why did that thought bother her, she wondered? It couldn't be because she would be leaving Jack Armstrong behind. She didn't even like the man.

Someone hooted at her and she realised her speed had dropped enough to annoy the driver of the car behind. She sped up again and, glancing in her rear-view mirror, saw him raise his thumb in congratulation. He also mouthed something that might have been 'good girl'. Concentrating on the road ahead, Serena managed to ignore him, even when he gave her a little toot on his horn before he turned off.

She'd had it with men for the moment.

The apartment was empty, which was a surprise. OK, so Chrissie knew her way around, she'd been born in this area, but where would she go this late in the day? Serena knew she was home earlier than usual, but if her mother had gone shopping she should be back by now. Silly getting worried, though. Her mother wasn't senile. Not yet, anyway.

Simon arrived while she was opening a packet of pasta. 'I got fed up with takeaway,' she informed him, 'so we've got pasta and salad for a change.' She filled a saucepan with water and set it on the stove, but she didn't light the burner. 'Mother's still out somewhere.'

'Oh?' He tossed his jacket on to the sofa and dropped his briefcase on the floor. 'Where did she go?'

'I don't know. Do you think something might have happened to her? It's getting late.'

Simon shook his head. 'I doubt it. She likes stirring you up, Serena. She always has. And you rise to the bait every time.' He poured them both a glass of white wine. 'Be thankful for a few minutes of peace and quiet.'

'Yeah, you're right. Sometimes you'd think I was her mother, instead of the other way around. We'll give her half an hour, and if she's still not back we'll eat anyway.' She sank on to the sofa beside him. 'I wish I knew what to do about her. I thought she was getting better, but now she's started seeing things. She actually thought she saw my father on television.'

Simon laughed. 'What? He's some sort of celebrity now? Besides, how would she know what he looked like?

She hasn't seen him since she left for America. He must have changed a bit in almost thirty years.'

Serena shook her head. 'Not a celebrity. Just some man in the crowd. It could have been anyone. I told you, she's completely out of her head sometimes.'

Simon put down his drink with a sigh as the doorbell rang. 'Talk of the devil.'

Chrissie came through the door with a little rush of cold air and the scent of Chanel, closely followed by Jack and Nina.

'They brought me home,' she said breathlessly.

Serena got to her feet with a sense of impending doom. 'What happened, Mom? Did you forget where you live?' She turned to Jack. 'She's not under arrest, is she? I don't understand what you're doing here.'

Nina moved away from the door. 'I'll wait in the car, Jack.'

'Calm down, Serena. Your mother's fine. We met her at the university and she said she was running a bit late, so we gave her a ride home.'

Serena looked from one to the other. She couldn't imagine what her mother was doing at the university, and she knew Jack wasn't telling her everything.

Chrissie looked guiltily at Serena. 'I was just looking round the park. I'll go and freshen up before dinner.'

As the bedroom door closed behind her, Serena scowled at Jack. 'What's going on?'

He raised his hands, palms out, and shrugged. 'You tell me. We had a report there was a prowler in the university grounds and when we got there, who should turn up but your mother. When I found out who she was, I said we'd give her a lift home.' He gave Serena one of his cool blue stares. 'But as I said once before, I don't believe in coincidences.'

She closed her eyes. Chrissie had only been in England five minutes and she was already causing problems. 'You think my mother is somehow involved in all this?'

'What absolute rubbish!' Simon looked as if he was ready to hit Armstrong. 'This is my mother you're talking about. Besides, she's only just arrived in England so there's no way she could have anything to do with what's been going on.'

'I didn't say she had.' Jack kept his voice even. 'But I find it hard to believe she was wandering around the university grounds on an impulse.'

Serena sighed. 'That's what she does, Jack. She wanders around places on impulse. She has nothing to do with any of this, so leave her out of it.'

'I will if I can.' He looked over Serena's shoulder as Chrissie appeared from the bedroom. 'It was nice bumping into you, Mrs Prescott. I have to go now, but I'm sure we'll meet again.'

Simon practically growled. 'You should know your way out by now.' He closed the door behind Jack with a bang and locked it on the inside. 'I'm beginning to really dislike that man.'

Chrissie shut the bedroom door behind her. 'He told me he knows you, Serena. How did you get involved with a policeman? Is it to do with that boy you saved?'

Serena knew she had to tell her mother something. 'Simon's apartment was burglarised. Nothing was taken, but we had to call the police.'

Chrissie shook her head. 'No, there's more than that. I saw the way that man looks at you. Have you been sleeping with him?'

It was on the tip of her tongue to hotly deny the accusation, because that's what it sounded like, but why should she? She was a grown woman, and whomever she slept with was none of her mother's business. To avoid a row, she didn't answer, but Chrissie hadn't finished.'

'Keep away from him, Serena. Never get involved with a policeman. You can't trust any of them.'

Simon looked at his mother in surprise. 'You sound like you're talking from experience. When have you been involved with a policeman?'

Chrissie shook her head dismissively. 'I didn't say I had. I don't like them, that's all.'

Serena laughed. 'That's a pretty sweeping statement, Mother. You can't possibly dislike every policeman in the world. I expect some are quite nice.'

'Not that one. He knows exactly what he wants, and he won't let up until he gets it. I've met men like that before.'

Which was probably true, Serena thought. When they first moved to America Chrissie had left her new baby girl with an assortment of child-minders, often overnight, but once Serena started elementary school, her mother seemed to settle down. She found part-time employment and seemed to enjoy the role of a working mother.

'What do you think Jack Armstrong wants then?' Serena asked, jokingly.

'You,' Chrissie said, as she walked into the kitchen. 'And if you've got any sense at all, you'll stay well away from him.'

Serena looked at Simon and shook her head. 'I told you she's getting worse.'

'I don't know,' he said uneasily. 'She may be right. I've noticed the way Armstrong looks at you, as well.'

Serena felt her face flush. 'The look you see is not lust, it's loathing. He doesn't like me.'

Although she did wonder, as she helped her brother set the table, exactly what Chrissie had against policemen. As far as she knew, her mother had always managed to avoid any police violations, even parking tickets. She only had to smile, and even the toughest of men melted.

★ ★ ★

'So? What was Mrs Prescott doing prowling around the university grounds? Did you find out?'

'Just looking around, she says.'

'And you believe her?' Nina shook her head sadly. 'You're losing it, Jack. That Italian girl is muddying your brain. I'm not saying the mother's involved with the student's injuries, that happened before she got here, but she must know something. Do you think Serena Conti sent her mother to the university for some reason?'

Not having an answer, Jack picked up the phone and dialled out, tapping his fingers on the table while he waited for someone to answer. 'You got the address for that Freelander yet?' He grabbed a pad and wrote something down. 'I'll love you forever, darling.'

He looked at Nina and smiled. 'We have a name and address, so let's pay the owner of the big car a visit.'

She looked at her watch. 'Now?'

'Nothing like the present — unless you've something better to do.'

Nina sighed. 'When do I ever. I had a better social life on Vice.'

Grinning, he held the door for her. 'I'm sure you did. Let's see if we can take Mr R J Gurnon by surprise, shall we?'

The house was on an estate near the docks. Jack remembered when it had been a Council estate. Now the properties were privately owned, each front door different, most with a fancy conservatory taking up half the garden. In a futile bid to be different, each house had finished up practically identical to its neighbour. Some of the front gardens were tidy, others full of broken bicycles and car parts. Black bin bags were stacked in front of each house waiting collection.

The door of number eighteen was open slightly and he could hear a child's voice. He rang the bell and a woman shouted something. The door was pushed wide by a small child who could have belonged to either sex. The jeans, t-shirt and trainers were universal. The hair short, pale, and wispy. The face smeared with food of some sort.

Nina bent down. 'Hello, little one,' she said, in a surprisingly gentle voice.

'Is your mummy in?'

'If you're selling something, we can't afford it, so you might as well go away.' The woman was a bigger version of her child, except she had a clean face and the gender was fairly obvious because she was heavily pregnant. She gave Jack a closer look. 'You're police, aren't you. What's he done this time?'

'We don't want to talk on the doorstep. Can we come in for a minute, Mrs Gurnon?'

'Sheena Evans. I take his name, I take his debts as well.' She waved them into a cluttered living room. 'I got to go out later. I work nights, but I can't leave until Rick gets home. Is he in trouble?'

'Is he usually in trouble?' Nina asked. The child had climbed onto her lap and was pulling at her large hoop earrings. 'Would you mind if we waited for your husband and asked him a few questions?'

Jack stared at Nina in amazement when she took off one of her earrings and put it in the sticky little hand.

'He won't be home for an hour at least,' the woman told her, 'and I got to put Kylie to bed and get ready for work. You can catch Rick at the docks if you want to speak to him.' When Jack thanked her, she shrugged. 'Tell him I need him to come straight home.' She took the child from Nina and handed back the earring. 'I'll get the sack if I'm late again, and I need the money.'

'I wouldn't put that earring back on,' Jack said with a smile as they walked to the car. 'That child was filthy.'

'When you're a kid, you don't care if you're dirty, and that woman's working nights even though she's about to have a baby any minute. I don't suppose she's got much time to worry about little things like a dirty face.'

They found Rick Gurnon without any trouble. He was the shorter of the two men Jack had seen in the Freelander. The dock area was busy with men unloading shipping containers, a couple of cranes lifting the big ones off the boats. The smell of fish was strong; screaming seagulls and the larger herring gulls circled noisily overhead, dropping down occasionally to pluck something from the ground.

Rick was unloading a small container, stacking pallets of frozen fish on a forklift truck. He saw Jack walking towards him and tried to cover his nerves with bravado.

'Seen you before. Police, aren't you.'

'Seen you before as well,' Jack said. 'Watching a girl, weren't you.'

'Don't be daft. We stopped so I could get some cigarettes from the shop. Me mate was waiting for me.'

'Took you a hell of a long time, didn't it. Couple of hours. That's a long time to sit in a car doing nothing. As soon as you saw us arrive, you took off like a rocket. Where is your mate? He works on the docks as well, doesn't he?'

The man avoided the question. 'We wasn't doing nothing. We was having our lunch in the car. We're entitled to a break.'

'Of course you are.' He looked around. 'Interesting place, this. Lots of ways to make a bit on the side.'

'You really bothered if I take a bit of fish home? I thought you got better things to do.'

'Oh, I have, but you fascinate me, Rick, so I'll be keeping a close eye on you. And tell your mate I'll be watching him, too.' He started to walk away and then turned back. 'By the way, Sheena says to go straight home, she's got to get to work and she needs you to mind the baby.'

The man's face flushed red with anger. He obviously didn't like the idea of the police knowing where he lived — or talking to his woman.

'How did you know his mate works at the docks?' Nina asked, when they were out of earshot.

'Just guessing. Gurnon didn't deny it though, did he? So it looks like I got it right.'

'What do you reckon he wants with the Italian girl, then? Apart from the obvious, and he's not likely to get any of that.'

'I think he might want his phone back. Those six numbers must be important for some reason.'

'If they're phone numbers, I need the area code to trace them. Besides, I don't understand why he can't just get the numbers sent to him again. Are you sure there's nothing else on that phone? If you're right, and the phone belongs to him, he almost killed our student for it.'

'If it *is* the phone they're after. Speaking of Liam Glass, I suggest we pay a visit to the hospital tomorrow morning. He should be conscious again by then.'

Nina climbed into the passenger seat of Jack's car and buckled herself in.

'I'm surprised he's not dead by now. He must have the constitution of an elephant. Every time he wakes up he gets knocked out again. I know he's young, and he was probably quite healthy before all this started, but how much more can the poor kid take?'

Jack started the engine and drove away from the docks, the noise of the gulls growing fainter. It would take a while to get rid of the smell of fish.

11

Chrissie waited until both her children had left for work before she let herself out of the apartment. She worried about Serena. She always had. Wherever she went guilt was only a few steps behind, following her like the man with the scythe, just as big and just as scary.

She checked once again to make sure she looked as good as she possibly could. Not quite so easy now, but the few extra pounds in weight helped fill out the little lines on her face. Or that's what she told herself. She undid the top button of her red silk blouse and pulled her skirt down to just cover her knees. She didn't want to look like a tart, but there was no harm in using what she already had.

Simon's father had disapproved of her going out to work, even though she had a degree in corporate law. If she worked, it undermined his ability to take care of his family. Chrissie adored her son, even though he looked so much like his father, but when Simon started school, she became bored — her looks unappreciated and her talents wasted.

Dino Conti was supposed to be a romantic fling, a small break in her humdrum life. She never intended it to go any further, but he told her she had the body of an angel and bought her bouquets of flowers. When he took her out to dinner it was always somewhere dimly lit with candles on the table, where they could hold hands without being seen. She knew it was because he didn't want to be recognised by someone who might tell his wife, but she could forget that for one evening. When she got kicked out by her husband and took off for America, Dino didn't know she was pregnant.

Now he did. And that made her nervous.

The email in her bag said Serena was

in danger. That was enough. Dino would know if there was any danger around. It was his job to know. And maybe it was that element of danger that had first attracted her to him. But not any more. She wouldn't let him involve Serena in his corrupt lifestyle.

She stood outside the entrance to the café and felt her heart flutter uncomfortably. She put a hand to her chest. What would he look like now? His hair was still black, she had seen that on the television, while hers needed a bit of help — but they were both more than twenty years older. Would she really recognise him in a crowded café?

Staring anxiously around, she almost missed the tall, dark-haired man sitting at a table in the corner. It was lunchtime and the noise level was several decibels too high, making her head ring. Elderly ladies nibbled on granary sandwiches while a group of students wolfed down fish and chips, talking at the tops of their voices. Everyone seemed to be speaking at once and for a moment Chrissie felt quite sick. Her appetite abruptly disappeared and she wished she hadn't come.

And then she saw him and her breathing stopped altogether. He was wearing a leather biker jacket and she could see his hair was now lightly brushed with silver. His eyes were concealed behind wrap-around sunglasses, but she knew what colour they were. The same chocolate brown as her daughter's.

He raised his head, and fear dried her mouth and stole the blood from her brain. She hung on to the back of a chair for support. She couldn't do this. Losing her nerve completely, she headed for the door as fast as her heels would allow, knocking into tables and apologising as she went. She wanted to cry. Even if he hadn't noticed her before, her panic-stricken exit must have attracted his attention. It had attracted everyone else's.

Reaching the street, she looked

frantically for a cab, but this was a small town in England, not the bustling city of Sacramento. The best she could do was hop on a double-decker bus standing at the bus stop. She almost laughed as she fished in her purse for coins. She didn't know where she wanted to go. She handed over a random amount of coins and took the ticket the driver handed her. Even her great escape was a farce.

Keeping her head down, she slid into a seat near the back of the bus. She had no idea how far the coins she had given the bus driver would take her. All she wanted to do was get away.

She had been fearful Dino would follow her and she waited anxiously for the bus to start. When there was no sign of him she began to breath again. But the bus stopped at a red traffic light a little further up the road and she saw him racing up to bang his hand against the closed door.

The driver wouldn't open the bus door, it was more than his job was worth. Chrissie thought she saw a smug smile on the man's face as he drove on, but she felt like cheering him. Dino looked furious, but if *she* had no idea where she was going, neither did he. She settled back in her seat and tried to breathe deeply the way her counsellor had shown her, and she felt the anxiety begin to ease. When the bus had gone a few more stops, she would get off and find her way home.

But the bus stops in the high street were close together and Dino could move really fast when he wanted to. He got on at the next stop and there was absolutely nothing she could do about it.

She watched him take a ticket and move towards her. He still looked angry, and when he slid into the seat beside her she cringed. He wouldn't hurt her, she knew him well enough to know that, but he still had the power to scare her. Without looking at her, he took the hand she had resting in her lap and held it in his.

'Why did you run away from me, Chrissie?'

Did he mean right now? Or twenty-three years ago? Both times she had chickened out. Up close, Serena was so like him Chrissie wanted to cry. Maybe she shouldn't have gone away without telling him, but back then he was married to an invalid, a woman he could never leave. Besides, a wife in a wheelchair was a good cover for his clandestine activities.

'Please look at me, Chrissie. I need to talk to you. Can we go somewhere, wherever you like. Out of town if you prefer.'

There was an element of pleading in his voice and she turned her head to look at him. It was no hardship looking at him — it never had been. 'You have a beautiful daughter,' she told him. 'She looks just like you.'

'I know. I saw her picture in the paper. Why did you give her my name?'

'It seemed the least I could do.'

'Yes.' He was silent for a moment,

looking past her out of the bus window. Then he shifted in his seat to face her again. 'She's in danger, Chrissie. She has something — I don't know what — but someone is prepared to kill for what she has.'

'I don't know what you mean?' Chrissie felt her heart start to race again. She had a mantra she was supposed to say when she was stressed, but when she was stressed she couldn't remember the words. 'You must tell me, Dino.'

He shook his head. 'I don't know. I'll try to find out, but it's difficult. I don't want to ask about things that don't concern me.'

Disappointment filled her. 'You're still mixing with criminals. I thought you'd have given it up by now, but I can see you haven't changed.'

He eased out of his seat and pulled her with him. 'We can't stay on the bus forever. Let's get off here. There's a pub I know.'

Yes, he would, she thought bitterly.

The ones he had taken her to before were always dark and slightly sleazy, but she had quite liked the idea of being a gangster's moll. So different from her life with Derek. With him she was a suburban housewife with a young son and successful husband, but in the dark confines of a dodgy pub she could be someone totally different.

Now, as she followed him through the door of The Spinnaker, she was pleasantly surprised.

A deck had been built out over the river and a few tables were occupied. He found a table in the sun and sat her down.

'Still tequila and lemonade in a long glass?' When she nodded, he put his hand over hers. 'I thought you might have picked up different likes and dislikes in the States.' He lifted her hand and turned it over to kiss her palm. 'Don't run away again, Chrissie.'

She watched him walk inside and a woman at another table turned her head to follow his progress. Nothing had changed. Except this time the interest in the woman's eyes made her smile, whereas once upon a time she would have been riddled with jealousy.

When he sat beside her on the bus she had realised he was wearing leather trousers as well as the leather jacket, so presumably he still rode a bike. He had once told her that for him it was the safest form of transport, because he was always in a hurry. Either chasing someone or trying to get away. By the time he came back with the drinks she had decided to sit back and enjoy herself. In a few days she would be back in America with Serena. Somewhere they would both be safe.

She sipped her drink. It had come without ice and unadorned with any greenery, just the way she liked it. But that had always been part of Dino's charm — knowing exactly what she liked. He was still beautiful. Tall, dark and handsome, without an ounce of fat on his lean frame.

'Why is Serena in danger?' she asked.

'All she did was help a student after he'd been mugged.'

'The student was pushed from a car, Chrissie. Deliberately. He must have given her something, or said something to her, and now bad men are after her. Perhaps she doesn't know anything, but you must tell her to think, to work out what she has that they want. And then tell her to give it back.'

'How can she do that if she doesn't know what it is? How are you involved, Dino. Are you working with them, the bad men? Are you putting your own daughter in danger?'

'No!' He shook his head violently. 'I didn't know who she was until I saw her picture in the paper, but even if I had, I would never deliberately put a young woman in danger. You should know that.'

She looked directly into his dark eyes, trying to see past the surface. 'So what is this all about, Dino. What are you mixed up in this time.'

He sighed. 'Smuggling. A dangerous

group with worldwide connections.'

'Drugs? You said you would never get involved with drugs!'

'It's not drugs.'

Her mind skittered. 'I don't understand,' she said. 'If it's not drugs, what is it?'

He sighed again and took some bank notes out of his pocket. Putting the money on the table in front of her, he got to his feet. 'I have to go, Chrissie. Give me a minute or two and then get a taxi home.'

'Please, Dino.' She caught hold of his hand. 'Tell me what this is all about. If it's not drugs these people are smuggling, what on earth is it?'

He kissed the palm of her hand again. 'Something much worse than drugs.'

* * *

When Nina and Jack got to the hospital, Liam was sitting up in bed looking reasonably normal. The swelling on his face had gone down and the bandage on his head was smaller. He even managed a smile when they walked into the room.

Nina glanced at Jack and then sat on the chair next to the bed. 'How are you, Liam?'

'Not too bad. Much better than I was.'

'How's your memory? Anything come back to you?'

'Some.' He took a sip of water, swallowing as if his throat hurt. 'Not all of it, but I remember the phone. Someone had left it behind.'

Jack was there immediately, bending down beside the bed. 'You found a mobile phone, didn't you? Where did you find it?'

'I went into the café for a coffee and a doughnut.' He twisted the plastic water-cup in his hands nervously. 'That's my usual breakfast. That little café just before you get to the uni gates. We all go there. Michael might have been with me, he usually is . . . but I can't remember.'

'And you found a phone?'

Liam closed his eyes as if he was trying to see that morning again in his head. 'No. Some guy left it behind. They were arguing, the two of them, and then they left. I chased after them, but they were already driving away.'

Jack was breathing down her neck, so Nina decided it was simpler to give up her seat. She moved out of the way and Jack sat down beside the bed.

'What were they arguing about, Liam. Could you hear what they were saying?'

'No . . . well, I probably could have, but I wasn't really listening.'

'So what did you do with the phone? Did you look at the address list to find out who it belonged to?'

'Yeah.' Liam licked his lips and took another sip of water. 'Sorry, it hurts my throat if I talk too long. Yeah, I looked for a list of contacts. I thought I could call someone. One of his friends. But there was nothing there.'

'Not anything?' Jack glanced at Nina. 'No numbers?'

Liam shook his head. 'No contacts list, no phone numbers, no texts, no nothing. It looked as if it had never been used — at first, anyway.'

'At first?'

'I went back to the flat, I remember that. I think it was to pick up some notes. I took the phone with me. I didn't want to take it to uni in case I lost it. It belonged to someone else, you see. I was about halfway there when it started to vibrate in my pocket.' He grinned painfully. 'Scared the whatsits out of me. Someone had sent some numbers. Probably a phone number, but it could have been anything . . . '

The student's voice was beginning to falter and Jack glanced anxiously at the door. Any moment a doctor would appear and tell them their time was up and they had to leave. 'So what did you do with the phone?'

'Took it back to the flat — I think I took it back to the flat. After that, everything's fuzzy. I can only see bits. I took my class. I'm sure I did. You can check my notes — or did I lose them? I think I hit my head on something. I don't remember anything much after I left the cafe.'

Jack smiled at the young man. He had done his best, poor kid. 'So the phone rang after you'd picked it up, and by that time the man who owned it had driven off in a car. Do you remember what sort of car?'

Liam shook his head and winced. 'Sorry. Get a bitch of a headache if I move my head.'

'Did you go back to the flat at lunch time?'

Liam closed his eyes again. 'I don't know.'

'We'll go now. You need your rest.' Nina gave Jack a warning look. 'You'll be no help to anyone if you have another relapse.'

Jack took the hint. She was right, give the kid a bit more time and he might remember some more. As it was, they had more than they did when they came in, even if it wasn't much.

They went downstairs to the restaurant for coffee before they went back to the station.

'I still don't understand,' Nina said. 'If someone came after him for the phone, why didn't he just hand it over. Why keep it? It was no use to him. He had his own phone.'

'We're presuming he had his own phone. No one's found it or handed it in so far.'

'I expect the two men who grabbed him took it off him. Besides, even if someone found it, they probably got a new sim card and kept it for themselves.'

'Why kidnap him, take him away in a car, and then sling him out on the road? This is lousy coffee.' Jack pushed his coffee cup away. 'Perhaps we're looking at this all wrong. There must be a logical explanation somewhere.'

'Maybe he's lying. Maybe he went willingly.'

'According to the hospital report, he was definitely knocked about a bit. No point if he went willingly. And someone either threw him out of the car, or he got out himself.'

'While it was moving.'

'Yeah. While it was moving quite fast. And if Liam lied to us today, he's probably been lying all along. Which means we can't believe anything he told us.'

Nina stretched long legs under the table. 'I think he's feeling too groggy to play games. Besides, he seems a nice kid. Sometimes you have to take things on trust. I know that's hard for you, but . . . '

'So we'll make two lists,' he interrupted. 'Things about the case we've proved to be true, and things that are pure speculation. Meaning guesses or lies. We could always do one of those storyboard things they use in movies. Pictures all over a big board on the wall.'

'You reckon they work? All the police

seem to do in American movies is look at pictures on walls. How does that help find the bad guys?'

'You'd rather go looking for them with a big gun, I suppose.'

She grinned. 'Of course. I've always fancied myself with a big gun. I wonder why they won't let me have one?'

'Probably because you'd shoot some-one.'

'Very true. So what's next?'

'You go back to the station and start making lists.' He looked at his watch. 'I think I'll give Miss Conti's mother another call. I don't believe Mrs Prescott is as daft as everyone makes out. She was hanging round the uni grounds for a reason.'

Nina gave him a sideways look. 'Drop me at the station then. I've got lists to make. And I'm sure you can manage the mother on your own. I'm sure you know the daughter quite well by now.'

'She's an important witness.'

'Yeah, yeah, yeah.' Nina finished her

coffee and got to her feet. 'We both know someone knows something. They're just not telling.'

'They will.' He treated her to his shark's grin. 'Believe me, they will.'

12

Serena spent the morning with Graham, showing him the basic principles of CGI. He was a quick learner, and after a short stop for lunch he only needed another hour on the computer to be fairly competent. Pleased with her teaching skills, Serena left him to play with the programme in his own time and headed for home.

When she saw the car in the car park she closed her eyes and sighed. She could do without Jack Armstrong right now, particularly if he had that leggy blond with him. What he was doing here at this time of day she had no idea. He knew she worked.

She was heading for the lift before logic clicked in. He must have come to see Chrissie. Maybe more had been going on when Jack and Nina picked her up than she had let on. Serena opened the door with her key, not quite sure what she might find.

Chrissie was sitting at the counter in the kitchen while Jack lounged against the door frame. Both of them had a glass in their hands and seemed to be on the best of terms. Serena felt a little flutter of trepidation as she tried to imagine what they had been talking about. It was probably a sign of insecurity to think they might have been talking about her. There was no sign of Nina, and for that she was grateful.

'Hello dear, you're home early.' Chrissie voice had a decided wobble.

'Yes. I'd finished what I needed to do, so I came home.' Serena looked at Jack, but his face was impassive. He was giving her enough rope to hang herself. Hard luck. She had no intention of letting him in on any of her family secrets.

Chrissie held up a bottle of white wine. 'Drink? We've got ice and soda if you want a tall glass.'

'Please.' Serena slipped off her jacket. 'I didn't know you were entertaining.'

That made Jack smile. He moved away from the door and half-filled a highball glass with Chardonney. 'Your mother is a good hostess. She knows a spritzer won't put me over the limit — not that this is an official visit.'

She took the glass he handed her and topped it up with soda from a can. 'So what is it, then?'

Chrissie was drinking her wine neat and now she took a long swallow. 'He came to see me, I think.'

'Why?' She couldn't imagine why someone like Jack would take Chrissie seriously. 'My mother isn't well, Mr Armstrong and I don't think you have any right to interrogate her when I'm not here to support her.'

'Oh, for goodness sake, Serena. I'm quite capable of speaking for myself. I may have had a breakdown, but it didn't leave me brain-damaged. I know for a fact you're on a first name basis with Jack, so why put on that prissy voice? There's something you should know, and it's probably just as well the policeman is here. Otherwise you won't believe a word I say.'

Because half the time you talk a load of rubbish, Serena though crossly. She knew what would happen, she would finish up the bad guy in all this. Her mother was an expert at laying the blame on anyone who happened to be around. She splashed more wine into her glass. She wasn't driving anywhere, and she needed something to calm the frustration she was feeling at the moment.

'What did you want to tell us, Mrs Prescott?' Jack asked affably.

He reached across to pour more wine into her mother's glass and Serena felt another flare of irritation. Loosening the tongue of the suspect before the interrogation must be a common police procedure.

'My mother's not a reliable witness. She takes Valium.' She winced at the look of hurt on her mother's face, but she told herself she was only doing it for Chrissie's protection.

'So do a lot of other people,' Jack said mildly. 'It's a medicine, Serena, the same as any other. It doesn't put an end to coherent thought.'

'I never said it did.' She hated the defensiveness in her voice. She was the bad guy already. 'Is this something to do with you picking my mother up the other night?'

He sat down on a kitchen stool and stretched out his legs. 'You tell me. I just called round for a chat.'

Like hell he did! She looked pleadingly at her mother. Whatever Chrissie was about to blurt out was bound to be something better left unsaid, but Chrissie had that look on her face and Serena knew there was no stopping her now.

'I met your father, Serena.'

She gave a snort of laughter. 'You haven't seen him since before I was born. I don't suppose you'd recognise him if he bumped into you in the street.'

'He got in touch with me. He saw your picture in the paper. Miss Serena Conti, a twenty-three year old on a visit from America. Dino hasn't got a history of mental illness like me, so presumably he connected the dots.' She took another gulp of her wine and set the empty glass on the counter. 'Besides, you look exactly like him.'

Serena stared at her mother. Could it possibly be true? She felt light-headed and grabbed her glass. She couldn't go all wobbly in front of Jack, not again, it would be too humiliating for words. She saw him looking at her as she tipped the rest of the soda into her glass. No, it wasn't possible. Chrissie made things up. This was just another of her stories. It had to be. A ploy to get the attention of an attractive man.

'I don't want to pry into private family matters, Mrs Prescott — unless it has any bearing on the present investigation, of course.'

'Oh, I'm sure it has, and please call me Chrissie. All that Mrs Prescott business makes me feel old.' She filled the kettle and turned it on. 'I need a shot of caffeine. If I drink any more wine you really will think I'm a crazy woman.' She closed her eyes to get her thoughts in order. 'Dino said Serena is in danger. Some men think she's taken something they want. He said she should give it back to them.'

Serena waved her hands in the air. 'This is ridiculous. Why would my father want to get in touch after all this time? And how would he know about the two men who've been following me? You're making it up, Mother.'

Jack leant forward on his seat. 'Yes, how would he know Serena is in danger?'

Chrissie moved deliberately slowly as she got instant coffee out of the cupboard and spooned it into three mugs. Serena knew what her mother was doing, she was stalling for time. Even if what she had said *was* the truth, she would never tell them everything. She liked her little secrets too much.

'He moves on the fringe. Always has. He knows this area well, particularly the dark side.'

Serena resisted the urge to snort again. 'What dark side? This is an Essex village, not the East End of London. You're letting your imagination run away with you again.'

Chrissie switched off the kettle, and for a moment she looked as if she might throw it at her daughter. 'Just for once be quiet and pay attention, Serena. Someone is trying to harm you. I don't know what it is you've got, but you have to give it back.'

Jack took the kettle out of Chrissie's hands and poured boiling water into the mugs. 'What exactly does he do, this man you know who moves on the fringe? Whose side is he on?'

Chrissie shook her head. 'I don't know. When I first met him I thought he was like one of the Kray twins, and I found that exciting. I didn't know him very long.'

'You knew him long enough to get

pregnant.' Serena tried to keep the bitterness out of her voice. When she was a little girl she had always wished she had a daddy, but it was too late now. The thought of meeting some strange man and finding out he was her father filled her with horror. She desperately hoped this was just another of her mother's fantasies.

Jack put a mug of coffee in her hands. 'The man in the house next door. He wasn't one of the two men who were following you. He didn't fit.'

'No!' Serena shook her head again, making her curls dance on her shoulders. She felt more scared now than when she thought two dangerous criminals were following her. 'Mom, tell him you're making it up.'

'I'm not making anything up.' Chrissie rummaged in her bag. 'I took a picture when he was standing at the bar getting our drinks.' She flicked through the images and handed Serena her phone. 'See, I said you look like him.'

Serena tipped the screen away from

the light to study the tall, dark man who was her father. If her mother had told him she was pregnant before she ran away, he might have come looking for his daughter. She was trying desperately hard not to hate her mother, telling herself she might have done the same thing in the same circumstances.

'Does he want to meet me?' she asked, blinking back the stupid tears that were pricking at the back of eyes. She looked up from the screen and saw the answer written on her mother's face. 'Did he say why not?'

Chrissie looked at her daughter helplessly. 'He doesn't want you involved in his business, Serena. It could put you in even more danger, and you're in enough trouble already.'

Jack took the phone out of Serena's unresisting hand. 'I need to talk to this man, Chrissie. You said he's worried about his daughter. So am I. We both want to keep Serena out of danger, so I have to talk to him face to face.' Before

Chrissie could protest he was pushing buttons. 'I've forwarded the picture to my computer at the police station. If he has a record, I'll find him.'

Serena felt sick. She had only just found her father and now Jack was intent on locking him up. She looked at her mother. 'Aren't you going to say something?'

'Believe it or not, Serena, all I care about is you. Jack has to do whatever he thinks is best.'

Actually, she thought bitterly, no one cared about her. She was going to have to visit her father in a prison cell. 'Great.' She scowled at Jack. 'I'll walk you to your car.'

He gave her a small smile and then turned to Chrissie. 'I've obviously outstayed my welcome, Mrs Prescott. If Dino Conti gets in touch with you again see if you can set up another meeting. It's really important I talk to him.'

Serena resisted the impulse to push him out through the door. She brushed a hand over her face and followed him out into the corridor. The lift was waiting, its doors open. She followed him inside. 'I need to talk to you.'

He pushed a button and the doors closed, the lift starting its descent. 'What about? You never do what you're told, so what's the point?'

'Can you just listen to me for one minute.' She gave him a startled look as the lift juddered to a stop between floors. 'What just happened?'

'I stopped it. You said you wanted to talk to me.' He moved closer, smiling as she backed away. 'You've got a tear on your face.'

She felt his fingers skim down her cheek and shivered. He always managed to catch her when her defences were down. She swallowed, looking up into those blue, blue eyes, and knew she was completely lost.

If she thought about it afterwards she would have to admit she met him halfway. She had always considered making love in a lift as slightly sleazy pastime. A bit like in a telephone box, but not quite as brazen. If it hadn't been for the fact that she was afraid she might lean on a button and send the lift down to the ground floor, things might have gone a lot further than they did. She had a vision of the doors opening and them both tumbling out into the foyer.

'Talk,' she gasped, when he let her take a breath. 'We need to talk.'

He groaned against her mouth and then reluctantly released her. 'If this isn't communication, I don't know what is.'

Pushing him away, she straightened her clothes. 'There's probably a queue waiting at the bottom, and we look as if . . . you know . . . as if.'

He reached for her again. 'If people are going to talk anyway, we might as well give them something to talk about.' He frowned as she pushed a button. 'Spoilsport.'

He took her hand in the car park and led her to his car. 'Next time I'm going to take you out to dinner and then back to my place. I much prefer horizontal to vertical. But right now we're going for a coffee and that talk you keep on about.'

She texted her mother to say she was going for a coffee with Jack, and smiled to herself as she fastened her seat belt in his car. So there was going to be a next time. She deliberately forgot she would be flying back to California in a few days. Jack had numbed her brain enough to make her forget most things for a while. One thought she was determinedly keeping at bay was the idea that she might be falling in love with him. It was just lust, she told herself, nothing more. A desire to get her hands on him that had turned into a chronic ache.

He put a cappuccino covered in chocolate shavings in front of her, and she tried not to let her emotions show in her eyes. People talked about a fine line between love and hate and she had a feeling she might have crossed it. No point in regretting it now. Once it had happened it couldn't be undone.

'So you think your mother is telling the truth?'

'The picture proved it, didn't it? She's right, I never believe her, and she's better now. I can't seem to get it through my head she's not still making things up.'

'I need to find out where your father fits into all this. If he's not involved, I can forget I ever heard about him.'

'But you think he is.'

'You know it was him in the empty house, Serena. You saw him as well as I did. I think he was watching you, making sure you were safe. At least, I hope that's what he was doing.'

She wiped froth from her mouth with a napkin. 'I don't know which is worse. Thinking it might be some pervert stalking me, or finding out it's my father.'

He reached across the table and took her hand. 'Stop worrying about it. If you hadn't stopped that night to help someone, your father would never have found you.'

'I don't believe in fate. I think we bring things on ourselves.' She looked down at the table and he let go of her hand. 'Besides, despite what everyone thinks, I didn't stop to help Liam. I didn't even know he was there. I knew I'd hit something and I thought it was an animal. I didn't like the idea of leaving an injured animal by the roadside.' She lifted her head to meet his eyes. 'If I'd known it was a person, I might not have stopped.'

'The only way you can find out for sure is to hit someone else and see what you do then.' He laughed at her stricken expression. 'I was joking, Serena. Of course you would have stopped.'

'So what's next? Are you any nearer finding out what those two men are up to?'

'I'm sure your father knows, but I can't rely on finding him. I know where one of the men lives, and I know he works at the docks, but he won't give out any information on his friend. I can hardly go round to his house and beat it out of him, much as I'd like to.'

'Where's the cell phone now?'

'In the lost property office. I told them to let me know if somebody came in looking for it, but I don't think we'll have a taker.'

She twisted her coffee cup in its saucer. 'The numbers appeared after Liam found the phone, didn't they? Whoever sent those numbers may not know the phone got lost. When did you last check it?'

He pushed his chair back and pulled her to her feet, kissing her full on the mouth in front of everyone. 'You are a very clever girl, Serena Conti. I should've thought of that, but I didn't.'

Once they were back in the car, he called Nina. 'Go down to lost property and pick up the phone I handed in. I need to have another look at it.'

He drove like a maniac to the apartment block and practically pushed Serena out of his car. With a hurried 'see you soon' he disappeared in a spray of gravel. It was quite dark now and she glanced around a little anxiously, but there was nothing moving in the bushes or watching her from the trees as far as she could see.

The first hint she had of any danger was a scrunching in the gravel behind her. Before she could turn round, something was pressed tightly over her mouth and nose. The smell was disgusting, sweet and cloying, making her stomach heave. She lashed out with both her hands and feet, but only managed to flap feebly like a landed fish. She felt the world tip and there was no longer any sense of up or down. The night was dark, the sky overcast, but now a different kind of blackness was closing around her. She tried to shout, but her tongue filled her mouth like a pillow and she thought she was going to choke. Her body flopped. Her bones no longer had any real substance and she slithered towards the ground like melting ice cream.

13

When Jack got back to the office, Nina had the bag ready on his desk. She watched him curiously as he took out the phone. 'Something I should know about?'

'Just a thought.' There was no reason to tell her the thought wasn't his. 'Someone might have sent another message since we locked the phone away.'

'Not if they were waiting for someone to contact them on that number.'

'But we don't know that, do we? I should have learned by now never to assume anything.' He held the phone up so she could see the screen. 'See?'

'More numbers. What is it? A date?'

'Looks like it.' He glanced at his watch. 'If it is a date, something is going to happen at the beginning of next week. Tuesday, to be precise.'

'Like what? It's probably the date of a V concert, or a party at some kid's house while the parents are away. Do you think you might be making more of this than it is, Jack?'

He knew what she was getting at. 'You think I'm paying too much attention to this because of the Conti girl? I never let personal matters influence my work, Nina. You should know that.' He felt a stab of guilt. Usually, he didn't let personal feelings influence his work, but this time she might just be right. Time to concentrate on the job. He flipped back to the first lot of numbers. 'We've been assuming again. What if this isn't a telephone number? What if it's something else altogether?'

'Like what?'

'If I knew that I wouldn't be asking you.' He ran a hand through his hair. 'Put the numbers through the computer. Look for anything that uses six digit number combinations. See if you can get a short list. We've got to work this like a jigsaw puzzle. Incidentally, talking of jigsaw puzzles, we've got another piece to add to the mix. It looks as if Serena Conti's father is involved, so you can check him out while you're at it.'

'First name?'

'Dino. Had an affair with Chrissie Prescott that resulted in a pregnancy she never told him about. The product of the pregnancy was Serena Conti, born in the USA twenty-three years ago. There is one child from Chrissie's marriage to Derek Prescott who is now deceased. A son, Simon Prescott, ten years older than his half-sister.' He grinned at her. 'That enough to be going on with?'

'And what exactly will you be doing, sir?'

He ignored her sarcasm and picked up the phone, putting it back in the bag. 'I need information, and this might just do the trick. A carrot for the donkey.'

'You can't hand over police evidence.

Not when it's already been booked in.'

'This is not evidence. It got booked in as lost property. I'll just be giving it back to its owner.'

'So what am I supposed to tell lost property?'

'Make something up. Your last job should have taught you how to lie convincingly.'

He could feel her glaring at his back and probably holding a finger up, but now he was on the move he felt one hundred percent better. He hated sitting around waiting for something to happen. And, if he was honest, he *had* let the Conti girl get to him. He seemed to have trouble keeping his hands off her — and that wouldn't work when she was still part of his investigation.

He found Rick Gurnon cleaning out the inside of a large container. 'Got time to talk?'

The man twitched nervously and swung round with his fists bunched as if he was ready for a fight. He looked even more nervous when he saw who it was.

'Just finishing up before I knock off. I can't stop to chat, I'll be late home as it is.'

Touchy, Jack thought. I wonder why that is. 'I won't keep you long. I think I may have something of yours. Something you've been looking for.'

Rick tossed the rag he'd been using into a bucket and jumped down from the container trying to look bored. 'Like what?'

'Like a mobile phone.' He watched the wariness leave the man's eyes to be quickly followed by a crafty gleam.

'Could be mine if someone handed it in. Mine got stolen. You got it on you?'

'It might not be yours, though. A lot of them look the same. Anyway, I can't hand it over without proof of ownership.' He took the phone out of his pocket and tossed it on the palm of his hand, watching the mix of emotions travelling across Rick's face. This was more than a carrot, he thought. Definitely more than a carrot. 'Don't worry, it was just a thought. The owner will have to prove it belongs to him.'

'How would I do that?'

'Oooh, I don't know. Tell me what the last message was, maybe.'

'How would I know what the last fricking message was if somebody stole the phone?'

'Can you think of any other way of proving it's yours?' He gave Rick a hopeful look. Oh, this was such fun! 'Of course, we might be able to do a trade.'

'Like what?' The wariness was back. Rick looked scared now, poised on the balls of his feet, ready to run. The man was a bundle of nerves and, once again, Jack wondered why. The loss of a mobile phone didn't seem important enough to warrant the look of fear in the man's eyes. He jumped, swearing profusely when someone dropped a crate nearby.

'Problem?' Jack asked, keeping his voice easy.

Rick took a grubby tissue out of his pocket and wiped it across his face. 'What sort of a trade?'

'Seems a shame not to give you the phone,' Jack patted his pocket, 'What sort of messages do you get. Text, photos, voice mail?'

Sometimes a carrot works like a dream. He saw a gleam of hope in Rick's eyes.

'Maybe some numbers. Or a date. Something like that. I've been waiting for a message.'

Jack could practically see the wheels turning as Rick tried to make up a plausible story. 'Numbers?' he asked. 'What sort of numbers? Like somebody sending you a phone number, or something like that?'

'Yeah,' Rick said quickly. 'The phone number of a mate of mine. He should've left a date on there as well.' He was trying desperately hard to sound casual. 'Big party sometime next week.'

Jack pushed buttons on the phone and studied the screen. 'Could be, I suppose.' He held the phone up in the air when Rick tried to grab it. 'I told you. It'll have to be a trade.'

'What do I have to give you? I've got no money.'

'Information.'

'Like what?'

'Like the name of this man.' He held out the photo of Dino Conti, waving it under Rick's nose. 'Know him, do you?'

Strangely, Rick looked relieved. 'I might. But I need me phone back before I tell you anything.'

Jack shook his head. 'Like I said, it can't be done. The phone's police property now and I need a good reason to hand it over to you. He held out the photo again. 'So, who is this?'

Rick took the photo and stared at it. 'Works here, on the docks. He's mighty friendly with the boss. His name's Dingo, something like that. Don't know his other name.'

'Is he here now?'

Rick shrugged. 'How would I know. I just do what I'm told.'

'Yeah, I'm sure you do. How about your mate? The one with you in the car.

He work here too?'

Rick fidgeted. 'He's not me mate. We just have a pint sometime. Don't know where he works. You going to give me the phone, or not? I need to get home to the wife.'

Jack considered walking away, he already had more than he thought he was going to get, but handing over the phone meant Serena would be out of danger. He passed the phone to Rick who looked at it in surprise. 'You're letting me have it?'

'You could have just walked into the police station and asked for it. Saved us both a lot of hassle.'

He watched Rick put the phone in his pocket and crawl back inside the container. When he looked at his watch he realised it was later than he thought. Nina would have gone home. She'd left Vice so she could have a life after work, and that meant leaving on time. For a moment he thought of phoning Serena, he liked the sound of her voice, but she distracted him, and now he was getting closer to the truth he could do with out unnecessary distractions. Besides, Rick wasn't going anywhere, not until after the date next week, and his visit to Dino could wait until tomorrow.

He climbed back in his car and headed for home.

★　★　★

It might have been two minutes, or half an hour, before Serena awoke. She was cold. That was the first thought that entered her head. Chilled right through as if she had been lying on the cold ground forever. Had she fainted again? No, whatever had happened to her wasn't a faint. She remembered Jack driving her back to the apartment and then . . . what?

A wave of nausea sent a tremor through her body. She tried to put a hand to her mouth, but although her brain seemed to be working again her hand stubbornly refused to move. She turned her head and winced as pain stabbed through her temples, the granddaddy of all headaches was blooming behind her eyes.

It was so dark — or had she still got her eyes shut? She blinked, her eyelids moving sluggishly. Now she was sure her eyes were open she tried gingerly moving her head again — and realised she was no longer outside. Outside was never this black. There was always a star or two, or the glow from a street lamp. She blinked again and peered into the darkness. A sliver of something less dark appeared to be coming from under a door — which presupposed she was in a building of some sort.

Something was still seriously wrong with her body. Nothing seemed to be working quite as it should. Her limbs refused to respond to orders and her brain felt like mush. At first she thought her hands were tied because she couldn't move them, but now they were coming back to life she could wiggle her fingers. Feeling around, she discovered she was propped against a wall, slumped like a rag doll, her legs stretched out in front of her. She reached behind her and touched metal; cold, slightly damp, and rough in places, maybe from rust. There was more metal under her feet.

Was she in a tin can? Some sort of human sardine? And if so, how the hell had she got here?

She stayed sitting, not sure if she could stand just yet, listening for any sound of life. The walls creaked when she moved, like an old ship, and she wondered if she was on a boat, but then something skittered in a corner and her body responded automatically. She was on her feet in a second.

She didn't normally mind rats, had even held one once, but that rat had been kept in a cage. And if there were rats there were probably spiders. She would take a rat over a spider any day, but she didn't really want to share her tin can with either. She reminded herself she was in England. The creepy-crawlies in Florida were far worse.

She headed unsteadily for the strip of light and banged as hard as she could on the steel door. After a few minutes she stopped banging and sat back down on the floor. She had expected the sound to reverberate like a drum, but instead all she got was a dull sound that wouldn't carry for more than a couple of yards. Whoever had made her tin can had built it well.

Now her eyes were adjusted to the dark she could see all four walls. She paced out the inside of her prison and decided it was about ten to twelve feet long by about eight feet wide. The size of a big shed. Perhaps it was a shed — or a garage, maybe, but there was nothing in it. The whole space was completely bare — apart from rats and spiders. Not that it mattered, working out what she was imprisoned in wouldn't help her get out.

She had no idea how long she had been unconscious, but she was hungry and thirsty. Surely her captors would feed her? There wouldn't be much point in kidnapping her and then letting her die of starvation. Although, if they were still after the cell phone she might be in a bit of trouble, considering she no longer had it. They must already know she didn't have it on her. No doubt they had searched her — she didn't want to dwell on that — so perhaps she could think up a fictitious hiding place and suggest she took them to it. That's what they did in books, and at least that would get her out of her tin can.

She walked to the sliver of light again and got down on her hands and knees. Was that daylight out there now? Surely she hadn't been locked up all night? She stood up again on shaky legs and started banging again, this time with a certain amount of desperation.

She paused for a rest because her hands were starting to hurt, and that was when she heard the faint sound of voices. It could be anyone. Someone come to rescue her, or her kidnappers. Should she shout, or pretend she was still unconscious? She pressed her ear against the door, or what she thought was the door, and heard the sound of children playing. They were closer now, and there was no mistaking the shrill squeals of young kids. She started banging again in earnest and shouting for help at the top of her voice, hoping they were close enough to hear.

When she stopped banging, she realised the sounds outside had stopped as well and her heart plummeted. But then a rather nervous voice said, 'Hello?'

'Hello,' she called back. A surge of relief made her legs give way and she sat back on the floor. She didn't want to frighten the children so she had to be careful what she said. 'I've got myself shut in. Can you open the door and let me out?'

'We're not supposed to be here,' a boy's voice told her. 'We'll get in trouble.'

'No you won't.' If they went away now she would die. 'Not if you rescue me. You'll be a hero, like on the telly. But I won't tell anyone if you don't want me to. What's your name, and how old are you?'

'I'm ten and my name's Greg. My brother's eight.' He was quiet for a moment and she hoped he hadn't gone away. 'There's a big padlock on the door. It needs a key to open it.'

She felt her bottom lip quiver — it hadn't done that since she was a child. She couldn't send them away to get help because they wouldn't come back. They were too afraid of getting into trouble. A tear ran down her cheek and she brushed it away angrily. Think, girl, think.

'Have you got a cell phone, Greg?' There was silence again and she banged her hand against her head. 'Sorry, I'm from America. A mobile phone?'

'No, but my mum has. I'm not allowed one.'

'Are you going home now? To your mom?'

'We're going to school.'

'I got locked in here last night.' She had to keep him talking while she worked out what to do. 'What is this metal thing? Is it a building?'

'One of them big boxes they put on ships. This part of the docks is where they dump the old ones. We're not supposed to come here. How'd you get locked in? Was someone playing a trick on you?'

'Yes, it was just a silly joke. Don't worry about it. But I need to get out now. Is there anyone else around? Can you tell someone I'm shut in?'

'There's no one here.'

She could feel impatience building up and had to bite her bottom lip to stop herself shouting at the boy. 'Can you go and find someone then, please. I want to get out of here.'

'I don't have time. We've got to go now or we'll be late for school.'

'What time is it,' she asked hastily. She still couldn't see her watch. It had a black face, which didn't help.

'Twenty minutes to nine,' he said

proudly. 'I can tell the time properly now so I got a watch for my birthday.' His voice sounded fainter. 'I hope you get out soon.'

'Wait! Please wait a minute,' she pleaded. 'When you get to school, will you tell your teacher I'm shut in here, please?'

'I can't do that.' He was even further away now and she could hardly hear him. 'We'd get into trouble.'

'No you wouldn't.' She could hear the desperation in her voice, but she knew they'd already gone. All she could do was hope Jack found out where she was and got here before her captors came back.

But that wasn't going to happen. About half an hour after the boys had gone she heard the sound of the padlock being undone. She heard the padlock being pulled out of the hasp and watched the door start to open. Could she run for it?

As she eased herself nearer the door she knew she had just one chance. She was sure she could run faster than her captors, but she had to get past them first. The door slid open a couple of feet and a short, red-faced man eased himself through the gap, blocking the opening and any chance of escape. He was quickly followed by the tall, skinny one. They both stood looking at her as if they weren't sure of their next move.

'Can I go home now, please?' she asked, wishing she didn't sound so feeble.

'Shall we let her go?' the short one asked. 'We've got the number and the date now so we don't need her any more, do we?'

'You're bloody mental at times.' The tall one had lank blond hair and pale eyes. 'You don't use your brain at all. We can't let her go until after the shipment comes in, can we, you idiot? She's seen our faces. She can tell everyone who locked her in.'

They were talking about her as if she didn't exist — or was already dead. 'Excuse me,' she said, starting to walk

266

towards them. She daren't show fear even though her legs were trembling. 'You can let me go. I promise I won't say anything to . . . '

The thin one hit her round the face, knocking her over. She sat down hard and her head went back with a snap, hitting the bare metal floor. She found out what it was like to see stars and wondered if he had broken her cheekbone, it certainly felt like it. Part dizziness and part survival instinct kept her lying still, hoping that would make him think he'd knocked her out. He kicked her in the ribs with a pointed shoe and she still managed to stay completely motionless. She could only cope with one pain at a time.

She heard the short one say nervously, 'Have you killed her?'

'Grow up, Rick. She must have hit her head on the floor. I slapped her, that's all.'

'Like you slapped that student. He finished up nearly dead.'

'Told us he'd left the phone in his

flat. Maybe I should have finished him off.'

Serena was wondering if staying still was a good idea, but she didn't dare move in case he kicked her again. Maybe if they thought she was dead they would go away and leave the door open.

'So what do we do with her?'

She held her breath, waiting for the reply.

'Leave her in here. That way, she can't talk to anyone before the delivery date. Someone will let her out eventually.'

'What if they don't?'

Serena heard the tall one laugh. It wasn't a nice sound.

'Then that's another problem solved. Once we collect our payment, I'm off somewhere no one will find me.'

'Shouldn't we leave her some food and water?'

Serena cocked an ear hopefully, but the skinny one didn't even bother to reply. She could plead, but she knew it wouldn't make any difference. She heard the door close again and the padlock click into place — and she knew they wouldn't be coming back.

14

Jack got into work early, but not before Nina. She was sitting at his desk working on her laptop.

'Hi, boss.'

Jack walked round behind her and swung the chair away from his desk, making her squeak with alarm. She caught hold of her laptop as it slid towards the floor and got out of the chair as fast as she could, nearly falling off her high heels.

She turned on him furiously. 'Damn it, Jack, you only had to ask.'

'No man likes a woman stealing his favourite chair. Use your own next time. Did you get the info I asked you to?'

Nina pulled a spare chair up to the desk. She knew Jack well enough not to stay annoyed for long. 'If you'd called in last night I could have told you then.

I tried calling you, but your phone was turned off. You're supposed to keep it turned on for emergencies.'

He took his phone out of his pocket and turned it on, looking at the screen. 'Was there an emergency?'

She sighed. 'No. But I did find out something interesting about Dino Conti, and I could have told you sooner if I'd been able to get hold of you. He's not a criminal. Never has been. He's a cop. Works for some sort of special branch, undercover most of the time, so no one's talking.'

Jack sat up in his chair. That *was* interesting. 'So, if no one's talking, how did you find out?'

She smiled. 'You forget, I also worked undercover most of the time, and I have contacts.'

'Chrissie Prescott thought Dino was some sort of drugs baron.' Jack grinned. 'It would be unkind to disillusion her, wouldn't it? Did you find out what he's working on right now?'

She shook her head. 'Like I said, no

one's talking. That number you gave me is quite interesting, though.' When he just raised an eyebrow, she grinned and held up four fingers. 'One, Liam Glass found a phone. Two, the phone belongs to a man who works on the docks. Three, on the phone was a six-digit number. Four, I checked and found out shipping containers use six-digit numbers for identification purposes.' Her grin grew broader. 'How do you feel about coincidences?'

His smile was as wide as hers. 'The same way I feel about fairies. When I caught up with Rick Gurnon he was cleaning out a shipping container, but what sort of illegal shipment would come in a container? Most of the containers are quite a size. So not drugs, unless they're sent with something else. Lets hope it's not a shipment of guns or rockets. That would be way out of our jurisdiction.'

'If those two men are as unimportant as you think, it's probably a couple ounces of marijuana hidden in a container full of fish.

Jack pushed his chair back and put his feet on the desk, his favourite position for thinking. 'I showed the picture of Dino Conti to Rick Gurnon and he thinks Dino works on the docks as well, a close friend of the boss man. How's that for a coincidence?'

'Up there with the fairies. What are we going to do now?'

'Watch Rick Gurnon rather closely, especially on the 27th of May, which gives us two days to get our act together. I don't think they've got time to change the date. Besides, Rick spun me a fairly plausible story about a party and then I gave him the phone back, so he thinks I bought his story. He was happy to give Conti up in exchange for the phone. Not that he knows anything much about the man.'

'Conti's cover is good, then. That's how it should be. Do you think Rick and his mate are killers?'

Jack shook his head. 'No, I think they're just small fry, but scared silly of whoever's in charge.'

'The boss man?'

'Whoever is in charge probably organizes it all from abroad somewhere. He's not our problem, but Rick and his mate are.' His phone buzzed and he picked it up and checked the screen. 'Hi, Chrissie. What can I do for you?'

'Is Serena with you?' She sounded anxious, and a little bit embarrassed for calling. 'I believe you took her out last night.'

Jack felt something cold course through his veins. He remembered Serena getting out of the car, and he remembered driving off again in such a hurry he just left her standing there. He should have waited until she was safely inside the building. 'I dropped her back at the apartment, Chrissie. We only went out for a coffee.'

'She didn't come home last night. I thought she was with you.'

The fear in the woman's voice mimicked his own feeling of dread. 'Stay where you are. I'll be right over.'

Nina took one look at his face and put a hand on his arm. 'What is it, Jack?'

He got to his feet and reached for his coat. 'Serena Conti is missing. She hasn't been home all night. Her mother thought she was with me.'

He tried not to think about anything while he was driving to the apartment. He needed information rather than theories, and Chrissie knew how to contact Dino Conti. He was the only person Jack could think of who might be able to come up with some information on Serena's captors. Sometimes he really wished he *were* allowed to carry a gun.

Chrissie met him at the door of the apartment. 'Do you know where she is, Jack?'

He shook his head, following her inside. As he walked in to the living room a man came out of the kitchen. The man held out his hand. 'I'm Dino Conti. You must be Jack Armstrong. Chrissie's probably mentioned me.'

Jack took the offered hand, as lean and hard as the man. Dino Conti had to be in his early sixties but he was built like an athlete with not an ounce of surplus fat on his tall frame. His jet-black hair was only lightly flecked with grey and he had a smile that would still turn many a female head.

'Yes, she has, Mr Conti.' He gave Dino a smile of his own. 'I also checked up on you. Information was surprisingly hard to come by. We all have our secrets, don't we?'

Dino frowned. 'I've never met my daughter, Mr Armstrong. I didn't know she existed until I saw her name in the newspaper. I came here today to help find her.'

'Yes, thank you for that. I appreciate it must be difficult for you. I'm hoping you can fill in some of our missing pieces. We know something is going on at the docks in a couple of day's time. A smuggling operation of some kind, I would imagine.' He waited for Dino to say something, but the man remained silent. 'Yesterday, I handed a mobile phone back to a docker who goes by the name of Rick Gurnon. On it was a six-digit number and a date. I believe the number belongs to a shipping container that will be arriving on 27th May, but I have no idea what will be inside the container. Any information you can give us will help enormously.'

'But will it help find Serena?' Chrissie placed herself between the two men. 'Whatever Dino has done in the past has nothing to do with my daughter's disappearance. This is here and now, and I want her back.'

'So do I,' Jack said quietly. 'But the reason Serena has been taken has something to do with the smuggling operation.' He looked at Dino. 'Where would they have taken her? And now they have the phone back, will they let her go?'

'I doubt it. Not if she's seen both of them. Why would they? But I heard Gurnon talking to a mate of his, Larry Nells. Nells is not a nice man. Look him up and you'll find he's got a record for GBH. He likes hurting people . . . ' He turned round when he heard Chrissie gasp and put his arm round her shoulders. 'I'm sorry, little one, but it is the truth.' He tilted Chrissie's chin so he could look into her eyes. 'He is not a killer, though.'

'They would have to keep her where she couldn't be heard.' Chrissie rested her head tiredly on Dino's chest and Jack wondered if she had been up all night. 'Serena wouldn't keep quiet for long.'

Unless she was unconscious — or worse. Jack walked to the cupboard where he knew Simon kept his brandy and took out the bottle. He poured a shot for all three of them hoping it wouldn't dull his brain any further. He felt the liquid burn his throat and then fill his chest with warmth.

'How did Simon react when you told him, Chrissie? I'm surprised he went off to work.'

'I told him Serena was still with you.

But after Simon had left I started to worry. She would have called me again if she intended staying out all night.'

'There is one place where they could keep her locked in,' Dino said. 'They put old containers at the far end of the dock and once a year they get collected by a metal reclaim firm. There are always a few gathering rust. No one goes there because that's all there is. Rusty containers.'

It made sense. And doing something was always better than doing nothing. He looked at Dino. 'We'll take my car. I expect you came on your bike.'

Dino smiled. 'You saw me at the house that night. I knew Serena might be in danger, because I heard she had something they wanted, but I didn't know what it was. I was just keeping an eye on her. Trying to keep her safe.'

'I guessed it was something like that.' Jack turned to Chrissie. 'Stay here in case Serena gets in touch — or someone else does. If you hear anything at all phone me or Nina at the station.

She knows how to contact me.'

Chrissie gave Dino a peck on the cheek. 'Go find your daughter.'

He kissed her back, a light brush of his lips over hers. 'Don't worry. We'll find her.'

Jack wished he could really believe that. He started the car and put his foot to the floor. If he got stopped he would just flash his badge.

'Take the back road,' Dino said, as they neared the docks. 'I don't want to be seen with you.' He turned his head to grin at Jack. 'Nothing personal.'

'No, of course not.' Jack turned on to the road that skirted the dock area. He glanced sideways at Dino. 'I know you're working undercover, and I guessed it's a smuggling operation of some sort, but I couldn't work out what's being smuggled in. This is an insignificant little port for a big smuggling operation.'

'That's what they want. An insignificant little port. Fish is the main import here, so the security is minimal. And you're right, something is going down in a couple of days. We know the date, and we know what's being imported. All we need is the container number.'

'I might have that,' Jack said. 'Tell me what they're bringing in and I'll give you the number.'

Dino smiled. 'A civilized exchange of information between police officers.'

'Something like that.' He turned onto a strip of unmade road with a sign telling them to keep out. 'Chrissie doesn't know what you do, does she?'

'She never asked. She thought I was one of the big boys back then. I was dangerous but exciting. She thought I was mixed up with the Mafia. That was why she ran away when she found out she was pregnant with our daughter. Besides, I was married back then.'

'Chrissie had to leave. Her husband kicked her out. She had a breakdown of some sort in America and Serena's been looking after her.'

'I didn't know that. I thought at first Chrissie left because of my associations.

And then, later, because I wouldn't have made a good father for our child.'

'What's the shipment, Dino? At least tell me that. I was hoping it was just a small shipment of drugs, but that sort or operation doesn't warrant the attention of an undercover agent.'

'It's not drugs. At least, I'm pretty sure it's not drugs.' He frowned. 'I don't think anyone knows exactly what the cargo is, but we've got an idea. Gurnon and Nills are too far down the food chain to be trusted with important information, they just unload the cargo and make sure it gets sent to the right place. We're pretty sure this isn't the only dockyard being used.'

Jack bumped the car over rough ground and came to a stop next to a scatter of old containers. Some with their door open, some with their doors closed. Most were at least twenty feet in length, but there were a few smaller ones. He got out of the car and waited for Dino. 'Is it safe to shout her name? We can't go around banging on each one. If she hears us, she won't know whether we're friend or foe.'

Dino looked around. 'It's open ground and quite a long way from the docks. This place was chosen because no one would hear her, and if Gurnon or Nells were here, we'd have seen their car. Make as much noise as you like.'

The containers had been dropped by a crane and sat at odd angles in an untidy double row. Grass and weeds had grown up between most of them. Jack couldn't imagine what it would be like to be locked up in one of these rusty monoliths overnight. He started walking between them, calling her name and then pausing to listen. Dino started walking down the second row.

Jack attempted to slide the door back on a particularly rusty box and then realised if the door was rusted shut, Serena couldn't be inside. He turned to the next one, which was open, and stepped inside. This was newer and the rust hadn't begun to take a hold. The inside echoed like a drum as he walked across the metal floor. Definitely a scary place to spend the night. Particularly if there was no guarantee anyone would ever come and let you out.

He stepped back out again as Dino called to him.

'I think she's been here, Jack. This is new.'

Dino held up a brass padlock and Jack felt his heart drop. If they'd taken her somewhere else, how would he ever find her? He took the padlock out of Dino's hand. 'This hasn't been unlocked, it's been cut. Why would her captors cut the padlock off? They'd have the key.'

Dino shrugged. 'If one of them lost his phone with an important message on it, he's quite likely to lose a padlock key. Besides, there's no proof Serena was here.'

Jack shook his head. 'Someone let her out. Someone who had to cut through the padlock.' He reached in his pocket for his phone. 'Damn, I left my BlackBerry in the car.' He started back to the car at a run, Dino a few paces behind, and grabbed his phone from the seat. He looked at the screen and then at Dino. 'I've got one missed call.'

* * *

Serena didn't believe in despair. It wasn't productive. Besides, she had seen her mother hit rock bottom and she knew how hard it was to find the surface again, but right this minute she felt pretty near the edge of that same black hole.

The boys wouldn't tell anyone she was here. She had told them it was just a game, so they would assume she'd be let out eventually. And kids that age had a built-in system that deleted unsolvable problems from their memory. Chrissie would miss her, but Chrissie thought she was with Jack, so how long would her mother wait before she checked to find out where her daughter had spent the night?

She caught her breath when she

heard a sound outside the door. Had the short man taken pity on her and come back to let her out?

'Is anyone in there?'

Relief flooded through her like a tidal wave. It wasn't one of her captors. She shouted back as loudly as she could. 'Yes! Can you get me out? I've been in here all night.'

She heard a scraping sound, and then the same voice again.

'I wasn't sure if he was making it up, but I bought bolt cutters just in case. Hang on.'

When the door opened she discovered she was crying. The man standing in front of her looked bewildered. 'Who locked you in? Greg's teacher phoned me. He said he didn't want to call the police in case Greg was making it up. My boy told his teacher he spoke to you this morning. He was scared of getting into trouble. He's not allowed to come this way with his little brother.'

Serena walked out with a hand shading her eyes. The daylight seemed particularly bright after the darkness of the container. She staggered a little and he caught her, this stranger who had come to her rescue.

'Shall I call an ambulance — or the police.' He helped her sit on a patch of weedy grass. 'I don't want to cause any more trouble for you, but you need to report this.'

He thought she had been shut in by someone she knew, because she had told his son it was just a game, although she couldn't imagine anyone shutting their friend in a shipping container overnight.

'No.' She shook her head. 'Just give me a minute and then perhaps you could drop me off. It's not far.'

'I'm sorry, but I can't just take you home and leave you. You need to go to a hospital and have them check you over.' He frowned at her worriedly. 'And you need to report this to the police.'

Serena wiped a tired hand over her eyes and pushed herself up from the grass. After a bit of a wobble, and a helping hand from her rescuer, she managed to stand on her own. 'I'm sorry, I don't know your name.'

'Bob. Robert Scrivener, but everyone calls me Bob.'

'Can you take me to the police station, then, Bob? I don't want to go to a hospital. I'm not physically injured.'

'You look as if you are. There's a big bruise on the side of your face.'

She'd forgotten she'd been hit. She put a hand to her cheek and winced. 'I agree I have to report this. If I need to go to hospital, the police will arrange it for me. Can I have your address in case they want to get in touch with you for a statement?'

He gave her a business card and helped her to his car. The drive only took fifteen minutes and she asked him to let her go in alone.

'I'm sure you have work to do, Mr Scrivener, and I don't want to hold you up any more, and thank you again — and your son. Tell Greg there might be a little reward for his bravery.'

'You don't have to do that.' Bob smiled. 'He still took his little brother somewhere he wasn't supposed to. But we might overlook that, under the circumstances.'

'I hope you do.' She got out of the car and went into the police station, knowing Bob Scrivener wouldn't drive off until she was safely inside. Unlike some other people.

Nina came rushing down the corridor to greet Serena. 'I'm so glad you're safe. Jack was really worried about you.'

Serena followed Nina into the main office. She got a few curious looks, but a black eye was a normal occurrence round here.

'Where is he, then?' she asked, as Nina pulled up a chair for her.

'Looking for you I think. He went bombing out of here as if a bear was chasing him.' I'll call him in a minute. Where have you been?

'Locked in a metal container down at the docks. You know about the two men who've been following me? They grabbed me when Jack dropped me off outside the apartment. He was in such a hurry to leave he didn't wait to see me go inside the building.'

'And I'm sure he's beating himself up about that. I could let him suffer a bit longer, but we ought to let your mother know you're safe.'

'She'll be frantic, and it's not good for her to worry. She's not well.' Everything suddenly caught up with Serena. 'Can you call my mother, please, and tell her I'm fine?'

Nina looked at her worriedly. 'I'm sure you're not fine. Did one of them hit you? You've got a real shiner. Definitely a black eye in the making.'

Someone came in with a cup of tea and Serena took it gratefully. 'One of them is a really nasty piece of work. He planned to leave me there and if no one found me, that was just too bad. He said if I died it was a problem solved.'

'Oh, you poor thing.' Nina took her hand. 'I wish I could take you home, but I can't do that. I'll call your mum, and then I'll see if I can get hold of Jack.'

'Do you have anything to eat?' Serena asked apologetically. 'I haven't eaten since yesterday and my stomach keeps making strange noises.'

Nina opened her drawer and took out a pack of sandwiches. 'I can get something else later. Coffee? Or would you rather have water?'

'I'd rather have a shot of brandy, but coffee will do fine for the moment.' She opened the sandwiches and took a bite without bothering to check what was inside. Plain bread would have tasted pretty wonderful.

She borrowed Nina's compact to dab powder foundation round her eye, and a comb to tidy her hair. There was no way she could get the comb through her tangled curls, that would take a metal-pronged brush, but it looked a lot better than it had. She wanted to clean herself up before her mother arrived.

Chrissie took one look at Serena and

burst into tears. 'I thought those men had locked you away somewhere and we'd never find you.' She hugged her daughter. 'Dino went with Jack to look for you.'

'They didn't find me. A boy's father let me out. He brought bolt-cutters out to the docks because he believed his son was telling the truth. Isn't that great?'

Chrissie smiled through her tears. 'I don't have any idea what you're talking about, but it doesn't matter. I'm just thankful you're safe.'

15

Jack put the phone back on the seat where he'd left it. He rested his arms on the top of the car and dropped his head between them. He took a deep breath before he looked at Dino. 'She's safe. A boy found her on his way to school this morning. His father let her out. God knows what she went through, locked in that container all night.' He breathed in through his nose. 'I'm going to find Rick Gurnon and that Nills character and lock them away for good.'

'You can't do that,' Dino said quietly. 'You helped find my daughter and I'm grateful for that but, like you, I have a job to do. If you pick up Gurnon and Nills that's all we'll get. Besides, they know nothing. My job is to find the organisation behind those two idiots.'

Dino was right. Serena was safely with her mother. 'So what now?'

'We wait. Sometime tomorrow a shipment will come in and you'll be there when they come to pick it up. You have to catch them in the act, Jack. At the moment you have nothing that will stand up in court. You can't even prove they had anything to do with Serena's abduction. It's just her word against them and, if you think about it, the whole thing sounds a bit farfetched. If it went to court at the moment, the defence would pounce on the fact that Chrissie has a mental health problem. Like mother, like daughter.'

'There's nothing wrong with Chrissie!'

'I know that, and you know that, but we're not talking about us, are we?'

Jack got back in the car. 'I'll get back to the station. Serena may have heard something that will help.'

'I'll wait a bit longer before I meet my daughter. She needs time to get used to the idea that she actually has a father. Besides, turning up at the police station with a police detective wouldn't be good for my image. Drop me back at Chrissie's apartment where I left my bike and I'll get back to the dockyard. I'll say I had a toothache or something. Don't worry; I'll keep a close eye on our two friends.'

*   *   *

Serena was making a formal statement when Jack walked in. She looked up at him and saw the shock in his eyes. She must look a mess. A glance in Nina's mirror had showed the bruising to her face and the already blossoming black eye. She knew she hadn't got the tangles out of her hair, and she was sure she must smell disgusting. She wanted to go straight home and have a bath, soaking for hours in every sweet smelling bath product she owned, but she needed to give a statement while everything was fresh in her mind.

He stood staring at her as if he wasn't sure what to do next. Serena thought he looked wonderful. Tall and mean. Full of anger against the men who had done this to her. Even if he hadn't actually found her, he had come looking.

She stood up slowly and swallowed a sob. She wished, just for once, he could forget his job and give her a hug.

He took a step towards her and the occupants of the crowded office held a concerted breath. Then he slowly closed the remaining distance between them and took her hand. 'I'm very glad you're safe, Serena. Finish your statement and go home.' He looked at Chrissie. 'And take your mother with you. She looks worse than you do.'

Chrissie managed a laugh. 'Thanks, Jack.'

Nina went back to her laptop. 'This won't take much longer.'

Serena finished her statement with mixed emotions. Jack had looked at her as if he wished he could do more than hold her hand, but he was, first and foremost, a policeman.

Jack looked at his colleagues. 'I'll need most of you working on the smuggling case tomorrow. There's an illegal shipment coming in. I have no idea at present what that shipment is, but we need to identify it and secure it before it gets taken off site. We also need to apprehend the men responsible. I'll get Nina to hand out copies of all the information we've got so you are all right up to date.'

He turned back to Serena. 'I might need you with me to formally identify the two men who abducted you. If we can tie them to the smuggling racket and your abduction, they'll go away for a long time.' When she nodded, he smiled. 'I'll get someone to run you both home and if it's not too late when I finish up here, I'll call round to make sure you're OK.'

'Don't let him in,' someone hissed from the back of the room. 'He's dangerous.'

Serena laughed. 'I know. That's what I like about him.'

Once she was back in the apartment, she spent half an hour in the luxurious bath she had promised herself. She knew it would take more than a bath to wash away the smell of the container, but the perfumed oils certainly helped. Wrapped in a fluffy robe that belonged to her mother, she collapsed on the sofa with a blueberry muffin and a mug of hot chocolate liberally dotted with marshmallows. She felt as if she was back home in Sacramento — apart from the fact that Simon wouldn't stop pacing and Chrissie looked like a spring wound up too tight. It was only early evening, but Serena had never been so tired before. She felt completely drained.

'Your father was here earlier,' Chrissie said. 'He wants to meet you.'

Serena pushed herself upright. 'When? Not tonight? I don't want to meet anyone tonight.'

'No, of course not,' Chrissie said soothingly. 'Whenever you feel ready.'

'You don't have to meet him at all,' Simon snapped. 'You don't even know the man.'

'That was my fault,' Chrissie said.

'He didn't know Serena existed until a few days ago.'

'It's OK, Mom,' Serena shot Simon a look. 'No one's blaming you.'

Simon looked as if he was about to disagree, but another warning glance from Serena shut him up.

The doorbell made them all jump.

'If it's him I'll send him away.' Simon let his shoulders drop with relief when he saw it was Jack, but he was still on the defensive. 'She's having a rest right now.'

'I won't stay more than a minute. We've got a long day tomorrow.' He walked past Simon and before Serena had a chance to protest he scooped her up in his arms and kissed her soundly.

Simon looked slightly shocked when Serena slid her arms round his neck and kissed him back, but Chrissie laughed. 'About time, Jack. You behaved like a prissy idiot this afternoon.'

Jack put Serena down but kept his arm round her. 'The place was full of my fellow officers, people I work with.

Besides, fraternising with a witness is frowned upon.'

Serena looked innocently up at him. 'Oh, so that's what it's called, is it? What you just did? Fraternising?'

'It takes many forms. Remind me to show you the others, sometime.' He looked at Chrissie. 'Dino sends his love, by the way.'

Chrissie's pale skin turned pink. 'Would you like a drink, Jack?'

He laughed. 'No, thank you. I have to go now. Serena will see me out.'

She stood unashamedly outside Simon's front door in her dressing gown and let Jack kiss her goodnight. He made a good job of it, and when he eventually stepped away from her he put his hand on the wall for support.

'I'd better go before I do something I shouldn't and ruin both our reputations.'

'I don't think I have one of those.' She smiled up at him. 'Can I take a rain check on whatever else you had in mind?'

He brushed his lips over hers. 'Go inside, Serena. I'll phone you tomorrow.'

This time he waited until he heard the bolt slide home on the other side of the door before he turned towards the lift.

★　★　★

It had been a cold, miserable day at the dockyard. Containers had been loaded and unloaded and Jack knew they hadn't missed any. He had a man posted down at the dock area, but the container they were looking for didn't appear.

Nina sat beside him in the unmarked car with a fleece jacket zipped up to the neck. She had Uggs on her feet instead of the usual heels, but she still looked cold. 'There are only two ro-ro bays, so whatever it is has to come that way, and they don't like working here much after dark.' She stuffed her hands inside her sleeves. 'The lighting isn't that good, and no dockyard can afford a serious accident.'

There were three other cars, with two officers in each, parked in strategic places round the dock, and he wondered if they were all wasting their time. He took out his phone and called the police sergeant down at the container bay.

'Nothing new,' Frank Potter told him. 'You think we might have missed it?'

'Or we're on a wild goose chase.'

Nina gave a little squeal when someone tapped on the car window next to here. She gave a little sigh of relief when she saw who it was and rolled down her window.

Jack turned in his seat. 'What the hell are you doing here? I thought I told you to stay at home.'

'You should know by now I very rarely do what I'm told. Are you going to let me in or shall I run around a bit out here to keep warm?'

'For God's sake, get in the car.' He

cursed again as she wriggled in and closed the door with a bang.

'I thought you would have it all sorted by now. What's been happening?'

'Not a lot. That's why we're still here.'

The next moment the rear door of the car opened and someone slid onto the back seat next to Serena. Jack threw up his arms. 'Hello, Dino. Did you bring Chrissie? The rest of the family seems to be here.'

Ignoring Jack, Dino turned in his seat to look at Serena. 'This is not the way I wanted us to meet.'

'Nor me.' She smiled at him, feeling ridiculously shy. 'We'll have to catch up later.'

'The container arrived sometime last night,' Dino told Jack. I don't think it got taken away. I think it's still here.'

'Last night? So they landed it last night, took the contraband out, and left an empty container for us to find today. Brilliant!'

'I don't think it's empty.'

Jack swivelled round in his seat to look at Dino. 'That doesn't make sense. Why would they go to all that trouble and not take the contents?'

'Because they don't need the contents any more. They've already got what they want. The price of the trip.'

Beside him, Serena shook her head. 'I don't understand. The price of what trip?'

Nina slammed her hand on the dashboard. 'People! That's what the shipment was. Not drugs or arms — human beings. They charge for the trip and then sell them — men, women and children — for cheap labour.'

Dino shook his head. 'Not in this case. We were getting too close, and they already had the bulk of the money, money that would have taken years to save. They could afford to ditch the contents. They took the container off the ship and dumped it somewhere out of the way.' He leaned forward between the front seats. 'The people in that container have probably been on that boat for days without food or water, and they may have children with them. We have to find those people quickly.'

Jack got out of the car and looked around helplessly. 'This yard can store over 2,000 containers at any one time. We don't even know what size it is. Tell me where to start.' When Dino said nothing, he phoned down to the unloading bay. 'The shipment came in last night after dark, Frank. Ask around. You have the container number, or at least part of it. See if anyone knows anything.'

Dino rolled down his window. 'Our two villains, Nills and Gurnon, are long gone. The wife came looking for him this morning. She seemed quite pleased when I told her he'd left.'

Serena got out of the car and stood beside Jack. They were parked on a slight rise and the newly landed containers below them were packed tightly together in tidy rows. Much neater rows than the ones where she had been kept.

'People would shout,' she said. 'When they got hungry, or when their kids got hungry, they'd shout and bang the door. Anything to get out. Being caught would be better than dying. If they were in one of those rows down there, someone would hear them.'

Jack turned to look at her. 'So they'd need to put the container somewhere secluded, to give Nills and Gurnon time to make their getaway.

'They told me if no one found me, and I died, it would be a problem solved.'

Jack jumped back in the car. 'Can you stay with us, Dino. We could do with the help, but I don't want to ruin your cover.'

Dino shrugged. 'It's over for me. I've passed on all the information I could and now it's up to someone else. I told Chrissie I'm getting out. I asked her to marry me.'

'Marry you?' Serena hadn't meant the words to come out as a yelp, but Jack drove over a particularly nasty pothole at that moment.

Dino looked at her. 'Would you mind so very much, Serena. I want your mother to stay with me in England, but she said you have to agree. She won't stay unless you agree.'

Serena thought it was strange that she had wanted to be on her own for so many years and now the thought frightened her. 'Of course I agree,' she said bravely, 'I think it's a wonderful idea.' At least her mother would have someone to look after her.

Jack was about to say something, but the old containers loomed up in front of him and he braked to a stop. It was getting dark, and the rusty metal piles looked quite menacing. 'Check for locked doors,' he said. 'Most of them will be open. And listen for any odd sounds. They'll be keeping quiet in case we're the port authorities, but children always make a noise.'

'They may not be able to make a noise,' Dino said quietly. 'Dehydration is pretty debilitating, especially for children.'

Serena was already out of the car, running between the containers, her heart pumping, looking for padlocks, scuffed ground, anything that might be a clue. She remembered how it had felt to be shut in one of the tin boxes just for a night, and tried not to think about a choppy sea crossing taking several days.

Dino found them. There wasn't a lock on the door so they could have left any time they wanted to, but they were waiting to be told where to go, confident their money had bought them a job and somewhere to live.

In the end hunger would have driven them out; or perhaps a sick child.

Jack phoned for an ambulance and Social Services. It wasn't his job to sort out the legal implications, and for that he was grateful. The moral implications were something different altogether, and might never be sorted out.

Serena took bottled water from

Dino's rucksack and distributed it as best she could, trying to explain to a woman with cracked and bleeding lips that she should only have a small sip. There were only two children among the twenty or so adults, both boys about ten or eleven. Old enough to work.

They staggered out in ones or twos and sat on the ground. Dino had also brought chocolate bars. Only enough for a few squares each, but better than nothing. Nina found a blanket in the boot of Jack's car and gave it to the smaller of the two children. The rest huddled together for warmth on the damp grass, refusing to go back into the container to wait until help arrived. Serena didn't blame them one bit.

It was well over an hour before she got back to the apartment and explained what had happened.

Chrissie hugged her. 'I'm just glad you're safe.'

Dino had followed Serena inside and now he wrapped his arms round both of them. 'Jack is sorting out the paper-work, then he's coming over here. I feel bad about being so happy. I don't know what will happen to those poor people.'

Chrissie kissed him. 'You can't be responsible for all the people in the world, Dino. It's time to care about yourself and your family.'

Serena wriggled out of Dino's arms. She had managed to endure the group hug because he was her father, but she didn't know the man, and being hugged by a complete stranger wasn't usually on her agenda.

'I'll make us some coffee,' she said, glad to busy herself in the kitchen. Looking after her mother, and worrying about her on a day to day basis, had become part of her life. Now she felt redundant.

Chrissie spent the next hour bringing Dino up to date. He wanted to hear about their life in Sacramento, and when Chrissie told him she wouldn't miss it one bit, Serena tried to work out if she felt the same. She remembered how cold it had been on the estuary and thought she might miss the sun, but when Jack walked through the door she realised sunshine wasn't that important.

He looked tired, and she wanted to rush over to him and take him in her arms, but instead she walked towards him slowly.

He didn't move. 'Liam Glass left hospital. He's gone home with his parents.'

She tried a hesitant smile. 'So everything's been sorted.'

'Not quite. There might still be a few loose ends.'

'Mom's going to stay in England with Dino. They're getting married.'

'I know. What are you going to do, Serena? Will you go back to America after the wedding?'

She stopped a foot away from him. 'That depends if you want me to stay here. And if you say it's up to me, I might just kill you.'

He still didn't move, but this time he did smile. 'You know I want you to stay.

I'd like to take things more slowly. I thought you were going back to America as soon as your job here was finished, so I probably rushed things a bit.'

'Yes, you probably did.' She looked at him thoughtfully. 'So, if I stay in England, we take things more slowly.' She took another step towards him. 'How slowly?'

Chrissie gave a very unladylike snort. 'If you take things any more slowly, Jack, we'll all die of suspense. Be a man and give her a kiss.'

Jack closed the space between them and pulled Serena into his arms. He dropped a light kiss on the top of her head. 'I'm saving the rest for later — when we're on our own.'

'When we can take things more slowly?'

'Something like that. I suggest we go out for a coffee.'

As they headed towards the door, Chrissie called after them. 'If you're staying out all night again, Serena, please let me know.'

'And remember, Jack,' Dino shouted as the door closed behind them, 'you've got her father to deal with now, as well.'

THE END